I Should Have Stayed In Oz

Edited by Selina Rosen

This is a work of fiction. All the characters and events portrayed in this book are fictitious, and any resemblance to real people is purely coincidental.

ISBN 978-1-937105-09-9

I Should Have Stayed In Oz First Edition Copyright © 2011 by Yard Dog Press

Individual copyrights to authors of these new, original works as follows:

"There's No Place Like a Gingham Home" © 2011 by Claudia Christian
"Expecting Oz" © 2011 by Traci Lewis
"Not in Kansas Anymore" © 2011 by Rhonda Eudaly
"Even Black is Bright in Oz" © 2011 by Trina Jacobs
"Silver Slippers" © 2011 by vickey malone kennedy
"A Bad Case of the Munchies" © 2011 by Susan Satterfield
"It's a Dog's Life" © 2011 by Melyssa Childs-Wiley
"Suffer Not a Witch to Live in Kansas" © 2011 by Steven-Elliot Altman
"The Munchkin Boy" © 2011 by Tim Frayser
"East of the Sun, West of the Moon" © 2011 by Tracy Morris
"Kansas Sucks" © 2011 by Selina Rosen
"The Monkey Queen of Oz" © 2011 by Sherri Dean
"Who Road the Winds" © 2011 by Bradley H. and Susan P. Sinor
"But Wait, There's More!" © 2011 by Allison Stein
"Oh, Them Silver Slippers" © 2011 by Laura J. Underwood
"Dorothy Down Under" © 2011 by Glenn Sixbury
Cover Art © 2011 Brad Foster

All rights reserved. No part of this book may be reproduced in any form or by any electronic or mechanical means, including information storage and retrieval systems, without permission in writing from the publisher, except by a reviewer, who may quote brief passages in a review. Any members of educational institutions wishing to photocopy part or all of the work for classroom use, or publishers who would like to obtain permission to include the work in an anthology should send their inquiries to Yard Dog Press at the address below.

Yard Dog Press
710 W. Redbud Lane
Alma, AR 72921 by 7247

http://www.yarddogpress.com

Edited by Selina Rosen
Copy & Technical Editor Lynn Stranathan
Cover art by Brad Foster

First Edition September 1, 2011
Printed in the United States of America
0 9 8 7 6 5 4 3 2 1

Table of Contents

Introduction by Selina Rosen 7
"There's No Place Like a Gingham Home"
    by Claudia Christian 9
"Expecting Oz" by Traci Lewis 15
"Not in Kansas Anymore" by Rhonda Eudaly 21
"Even Black is Bright in Oz" by Trina Jacobs 31
"Silver Slippers" by vickey malone kennedy 35
"A Bad Case of the Munchies" by Susan Satterfield 45
"It's a Dog's Life" by Melyssa Childs-Wiley 53
"Suffer Not a Witch to Live in Kansas"
    by Steven-Elliot Altman 59
"The Munchkin Boy" by Tim Frayser 77
"East of the Sun, West of the Moon" by Tracy Morris 79
"Kansas Sucks" by Selina Rosen 91
"The Monkey Queen of Oz" by Sherri Dean 99
"Who Road the Winds" by Bradley H. and Susan P. Sinor 107
"But Wait, There's More!" by Allison Stein 121
"Oh, Them Silver Slippers" by Laura J. Underwood 125
"Dorothy Down Under" by Glenn Sixbury 133
About the Cover Artist 146

Kansas Really!
Selina Rosen

The idea for this anthology came about as so many of my ideas do. That's right; I needed to make some money. We're in the middle of an economic depression at a time when people are reading less to begin with and then there is the big move from print to EBooks which is just shaking everything up and no one's really sure where it's taking us. In the last twelve years everything about the publishing biz has changed, that's for sure.

Yard Dog Press is a different sort of publishing house, and things that don't work for other houses *do* work for us. Among those things are anthologies. The house could use a monetary shot in the arm, so an anthology was a good idea, but what to do? Not another *Bubbas of the Apocalypse* anthology; it's time to let that universe rest for awhile. But what then? It had to be something that YDP fans would like. It had to be something we could market. We can't take chances in the current market, so we needed a sure bet.

A concept with a widespread appeal is important. People are looking for a little escapism right now because the world has once again become a big, scary place, and few of us can really be sure of anything. We're looking for something to take our minds off our problems.

In short, we're all looking for a place where there isn't any trouble. And that's when it hit me. We all love *The Wonderful Wizard of OZ* and its message that no matter how fantastic the places we go may be— *There is no place like home.*

But we live in a time where our homes aren't secure. Debt and weather can snatch everything we've worked for away in a heart beat. We all feel a little beat up, vulnerable, and tired. Not unlike an orphaned girl living in Kansas.

Think about where the book starts—Kansas farming country— flat, gray, and dull. Dorothy isn't in an ideal position. She is staying with Aunt Em and Uncle Henry, but they aren't really family. Toto seems to be the only real friend she has. A tornado whips through and takes her, the dog, and the house far away to a place where everything is very different and filled with wonder and color—but also danger. She longs to go back to what's familiar.

Why?

I think that's where we all are now. Everything has been stirred up and set on its ear. It's very different, not terribly comfortable, and we'd just like to go back to the way things were before everything went to hell in a hand basket.

But like the old saying goes, you can never go home. And why would Dorothy want to go home? In Oz she was able to fight beasts, she was empowered, she made things happen, freed entire races from tyranny. What if upon returning home Dorothy began to realize that she never should have left Oz in the first place? What if she suddenly realized that coming home was a really big mistake?

Now a bunch of you are going to say, "We know Dorothy goes back to Oz because L. Frank Baum wrote many other Oz books." But let's face it, for most of the world—because of the play and the movie—we have only ever read that first book. I'd go so far as to say a great many people *only* know the play and movie, which were based on the first book. (If you have only seen the play and/or movie, some of the things in these stories will be new to you. Just know the writers did their research.) It is for this reason that I decided we would write these stories as if only the first book existed. Besides, it's been in the public domain since 1956.

The writers have taken this concept in many different directions, attacking the concept sometimes with comedy, others with dark irony, and sometimes delving into the deepest recesses of the human soul, but always with a certain reverence for a timeless classic.

Our world is different than it was twelve years ago. I'd go so far as to say as different in some ways as going from Kansas to Oz. Who knows? If we put our minds and hearts into it, click our heels together three times, and wish hard enough, it might all actually wind up better. We can only dream, and that's what *The Wonderful Wizard of Oz* was all about.

There's No Place Like a Gingham Home
Claudia Christian

The ratty old gingham couch creaked as Dorothy lifted her fossil-like butt to readjust the faded, too-tight gingham dress she had on. Gingham. God how she hated the fucking fabric. Fucking gingham…all of the men wanted her in "the dress," and now they demanded that her whole house be full of it.

"What kind of a fetish is this?" she mumbled as she scratched her moist wig. She adjusted the web cam so that it was ever-so-slightly out of focus and reapplied the Vaseline on the tiny camera lens. Sitting back again she drew a long suck out of an unfiltered menthol cigarette and gulped a glass of sweet tea with Kentucky Bourbon liberally floating in it. Toto number five noisily licked his nether regions where he lay on his miniature gingham bed in the dust-bunny-filled corner near the old black and white TV.

"Cool it Toto, Momma's gotta work now."

Dorothy took a deep breath, stubbed out the cigarette, readjusted her saggy tits, and jabbed a couple of keys on the yellowing keyboard.

"Hello handsome, how are you on this fine, hot day?"

Dorothy carefully forced a sexy smile onto her eighty-nine-year-old face, the tape holding her folds of skin tucked into the wig could fall if she moved too much, fucking humidity. A juniper colored, basset-hound of a face greeted her on the ancient PC's screen.

"Why, is that really YOU? Hot damned! You look exactly the same! Oh Dorothy, I used to play myself silly watching you when I was a boy…you were my ultimate fantasy, I can't even believe I'm talking to you!"

Dorothy saw some movement as the man started reaching south and tugging furiously at his Mr. Tin.

Good Lord what the hell am I doing at my age getting geezers off for $19.99 a chat?

"So, big boy…are you a lion in the sack or a straw man who likes to be poked with a pitch fork?"

The man stared wheezing and stammered

"I like it a little rough to tell you the truth Dorothy...will you spank me?"

Of course, she thought with resignation, *they all want Dorothy to be in control.* You'd think they'd want a sweet, innocent Dorothy, but nope, the pervs wanted her to act like some busty blond from a Nazi film!

The government was to blame. The second that social security was abolished Dorothy didn't have a hope in hell of surviving unless she used her female skills. God, it sucked.

Toto 5 snored and kicked his legs, chasing a car in his dog dream, so Dorothy had to speak louder.

"You know what you are?" She angled her face to its good side, if you could call it that.

"What am I?' the wobbly face turned an even brighter shade of red.

"You are a horrible man. You deserve to be punished...oh yeah I am going to spank you with the witch's broom and then I am going to slowly stick it..."

The screen went blank. Dorothy punched a few keys and banged the top of the computer. Suddenly the room went black, too. She heard the fridge rumble off and the air-conditioner come to a halt, and then the house was utterly quiet.

"Shit!"

Toto 5 grumbled awake and looked around the night-filled room, wondering what the fuss was about.

A sharp knock on the door penetrated the silence. Dorothy jumped a little then pushed herself off of the couch and shuffled to the front door in her gingham slippers.

"Who is it?"

"Open the door, Ma'am, it's Detective Butterworth"

"I don't know any Detective Butterworth. What do you want?"

"I just need to ask you a few questions, Dorothy. Please open the door."

"I don't have any lights; the electricity went out."

"I know. Just open the door."

Dorothy unloosed the rusty chain on the top of the door and unlocked the myriad of extra locks she'd had installed after the last hurricane. Her arthritic hands fumbled as the last of the locks jangled open. She opened the door a few inches and there he was, the same fellow who was on the computer screen just moments before! The front porch light was still on, its solar-powered orange light bulb casting a strange glow over his face.

"You're the ....weren't you just..."

"Yes, Ma'am. May I come in?"

Dorothy looked into his eyes. He didn't look smarmy after all, he looked kind and concerned. She opened the door all the way and let him enter her shabby sitting room.

Detective Butterworth looked around the dimly-lit room with its threadbare furnishings and smell of old people, dog, mothballs and hard-boiled eggs. He looked at the bunched-up old lady with the slightly-askew wig and motioned for her to sit on her couch. He took the chair across from her and sat on something hard.

"Oh!" He reached under his butt and came up with an old bone. They shared a little laugh and the ice broke.

"That's Toto number 5's bone, sorry 'bout that."

"No worries, Miss Dorothy. I'm here on some official business, which I am not terribly happy about but it's my job. I have the utmost respect for you, and I realize that times have been tough for a lot of people and they have to do what they have to do."

Detective Butterworth looked around, avoiding Dorothy's rheumy blue eyes.

"What's the problem, Detective?"

Detective Butterworth sucked in his breath and looked Dorothy straight in the eye.

"Ma'am, I'm not sure if you are aware of the law, but you are actively breaking it."

"What?! Whatever do you mean?"

"Phone sex. It's illegal here in Munchkinland."

"Since when?"

"Last year. The mayor of Munchkinland passed a law prohibiting it. The Munchkims were getting out of control again, just like the sex riots of '58. He's cracked down on any and all illicit sexual activities and businesses. I didn't want to be a part of this sting; I told them that you were a good lady......"

Dorothy fell back into the couch, stunned. The room was getting smaller. She forgot to breathe.

"Are you okay, Ma'am?"

Dorothy couldn't meet his eyes.

"What am I supposed to do now?" she croaked, a tear falling onto her gingham apron. "Am I going to jail?"

"No, of course not! I just have to give you a warning, not even a fine. It's your first offence, and I'll tell them you had no idea that the law was passed. It'll be fine."

"What am I supposed to do now? I don't even have electricity!"

"Oh, sorry. I can fix that…"

The detective heaved his lumpy body out of the chair and went outside. Dorothy heard a few grunts and exertion, then suddenly the lights went on. Toto 5 popped his head up and the Detective came back in wiping his hands on his wrinkled pants.

"I wasn't sure you would let me in so I flipped the power off, sorry about that. I didn't mean to scare you."

"Well that was pretty shitty of you. Why the hell would you want me in the dark?"

"Actually I did it because I was embarrassed to be here. I'm sorry, Miss Dorothy, but I have admired you for years. You're a hero to me. I told my Captain that I did not want this commission, but he made me do it. I didn't want to see your face when I slapped the warning on you."

The Detective looked sheepish and sincere. Dorothy's brain suddenly perked up; an idea was brewing in between the cobwebs and worries. She sat a little straighter and subtly straightened her wig. Moistening her lips, she gave her best come-hither look to the pudgy, vulnerable man.

"Well, that's all right, Detective, I know you were just doing your job… Unfortunately I don't have that right anymore… to a job I mean…"

She gave him as direct a look as she could through her cataract-ridden eyes. He heard the strength in her voice and looked up at her. Their eyes connected and something unspoken was suddenly clear as day. The Detective started to sweat a little, his face turning pinkish. Dorothy licked her lips and leaned forward.

"I wonder, Detective… I'm a little angry about this whole thing… Do you think someone should be punished for it?"

Detective Butterworth looked at the outstretched, age-spot-mottled hand and she could tell he knew that life would never be the same. He sat still for a moment, absorbing the electricity in the air, then he slowly reached into his pocket and pulled out his wallet. He handed the crisp fifty-dollar bill to Dorothy and got up off the couch. His knees creaked as he got on his hands and knees. Dorothy stood up, suddenly invigorated. She reached under the cushions of the couch and pulled out her lucky charm. Its weight felt good in her hands, she wielded it like the fellow with the light saber in the Star Wars movies. She flipped it around and put the stick end up against the Detective's buttocks.

This witches' broom was going to fly high tonight.

About the Author

"I guess you could say I'm the ultimate hyphen," laughs Claudia Christian. "I'm an actress - writer - singer - songwriter - director - producer - voice over artist – chef, and I'm sure there's a few more monikers I'm forgetting!"

She landed her first TV series at 18 on NBC's nighttime drama *Berringers* and her first studio feature at 20 playing a male alien trapped in a stripper's body in New Line Cinema's cult hit *The Hidden*. Claudia went on to star in studio pictures such as *Clean and Sober* with Morgan Freeman and Michael Keaton and *Hexed*, a Columbia Pictures black comedy that Christian counts as one of her favorite roles. Over 50 films and hundreds of TV shows later, Claudia has worked with George Clooney, Sharon Stone, Charlie Sheen, Nicolas Cage and countless other luminaries.

In addition to her acting credits Claudia has made 5 albums with acts such as the Award-winning band "Bubble" to her Babylon 5 costar Bill Mumy. She has also provided the voice for Helga Sinclair in Disney's feature film *Atlantis* and was the voice of Jaguar cars for many years. She has also won the golden headset award for her portrayal of Anne Manx in the award-winning series of audio books. She has provided voice matches for Jennifer Saunders in the Shrek games and has given voice to many more characters in games, features and cartoons.

Claudia moved to London in 2005 and immediately was cast in the BBC comedy *Broken News*. She also starred in the independent Sci-Fi comedy series *Star Hyke*. In August of 2006, Claudia debuted on stage in her first UK play, *Killing Time*, at the world-famous Edinburgh festival. She was rewarded for her efforts with a best actress nomination. She also starred in the American debut of Michael Weller's intense drama *What the Night Is For*, a role, which garnered her a Garland award.

In June 2007 Yard Dog Press published an account of her life to date titled *My Life With Geeks and Freaks* which she wrote as a thank you to her sci fi fans. On the fiction side of things, in May 2007, she had two short stories published by Under the Moon.

In 2010 Claudia starred in the Showtime series *Look*, based on the Adam Rifkin movie of the same name. It received great reviews and high ratings and highlighted Claudia's comedic abilities.

In 2011 she starred in the indie film *Leashed* with Chad Lowe.

She is currently finishing an epic Novo Romano novel with her writing partner, Morgan Grant Buchanan. Claudia is represented by Frank Weiman at The Literary Group in NY.

Claudia is also writing another non fiction book about Hollywood and The Sinclair Method which will be published by BenBella in 2012. She is represented by Launch Books Literary Agency for that work.

Expecting Oz
Traci Lewis

Glenda leaned forward with that magical gleam in her eyes and fixated on Dorothy. The girl concentrated hard on her gaze in an attempt to make out the words falling from the witch's mouth. Her thoughts were interrupted by the Scarecrow to her right.

"Come on Dorothy, breathe!" he instructed, twisting his lips.

Dorothy tried hard to get her mouth in the right position, to try and suck in air, but she couldn't. Her body writhed in intense pain. She started to cry as Glenda assured her everything would be okay.

What was going on? She sat propped up on large bed, several pillows elevating the upper half of her body. Dorothy squeezed the bed sheets as she was finally able to make out the directions the good witch was relaying.

"PUSH, DOROTHY, PUSH...."

She felt a swift kick to her gut and shot straight up in her tiny twin bed, a bead of sweat escaping the corner of her eyebrow. She sucked in the cool night air and tried to focus her eyesight.

"It was just a dream," she muttered. "Just a dream"

She looked down at her belly. Unfortunately, the entire dream hadn't been a figment of her imagination. She was still very pregnant as the baby reminded her again with another stout kick. She lay back down and tried to slow her racing heart.

Things hadn't exactly turned out the way Dorothy had wished they would that fateful day she had clicked her heels to come home from Oz.

Home wasn't exactly what she had returned to. She had expected Henry and Em would be happy to have her back, but her wild tales of yellow brick roads and evil melting witches had not gone over well. They shrugged them off as wild tales from a child with a very active imagination who had been traumatized by a tornado.

But Dorothy knew the truth. She wasn't crazy. Unfortunately they didn't see it that way. They decided they were not suited to deal with the situation and believed Dorothy needed professional help.

Em and Henry surrendered her to an orphanage. Dorothy bounced around several homes, not feeling exactly welcome or like she belonged anywhere. Toto was the only friend she'd had in the world. Now, Toto was gone. She had been forced to leave him behind with Em and Henry.

In the few years since she had returned from Oz she had dealt with things far too complicated for a teenager. Being an orphan didn't always bring you into contact with good, loving people, and Dorothy quickly learned she had to look out for herself because no one else would.

There was the alcoholic who had teased Dorothy by swinging an axe in her direction and saying he was the Tin Woodsman. Then there was the loony lady who claimed to be a prophet of God. She had believed Oz existed, but she also kept a pet cow in the house claiming its teats produced "holy liquid."

All Dorothy wanted to do was go back to Oz. She just didn't know how.

Things snowballed at the home of James and Willa Riversong, her third home in five years. There she met Jimmy, their strapping, young son. Four years her senior, Jimmy showed Dorothy things her virgin eyes had never seen. He taught her how to roll a cigarette and was even nice enough to teach her how to shoot whiskey.

They spent long nights up in the hay loft of the barn just talking, smoking, and emptying bottles. She felt like she finally had a friend. He believed her stories of Oz and offered to help her try and figure out how to get back there.

One night when they were up in the loft Jimmy asked if he could kiss her. When she told him she'd never been kissed before he offered to teach her how. Dorothy discovered her sensitive gag reflex that night when Jimmy shoved his tongue down her throat. She felt as though her own tongue was swimming in a pool of Jimmy's saliva. She didn't like kissing. So Jimmy offered to show her something that wouldn't involve their mouths.

Now Dorothy wasn't very worldly, but she was pretty sure what Jimmy was proposing wasn't right. But he assured her that as long as he didn't put it all the way in, nothing bad would happen. She believed him. It hurt like hell, and the sounds escaping Jimmy's mouth terrified her. He sounded like a coyote in heat.

"How do you like that, huh?" he whimpered. "Tell me I'm bigger than the lion, baby." As he reached climax he cried out, "My munchkin laid the yellow brick road!" When he was done Dorothy immediately felt dirty.

He made her promise not to tell, and from then on they didn't spend any more nights in the loft. In fact, Jimmy hardly paid any attention to her. He was busy with the next-door-neighbor's daughter, Sally. Sally had big boobs and curly, blonde hair. Dorothy was flat-chested and couldn't compete with the busty blonde. She was crushed but a little relieved, too.

It was only a few weeks later that Dorothy began to notice a change in her body. She couldn't keep anything down and nothing seemed to fit any more. She tried to hide the bulge in her belly, but it didn't take long for the Riversongs to catch on. Her excuse of Immaculate Conception didn't go over very well. Dorothy then tried to explain what happened, but Jimmy denied everything. They were appalled that Dorothy had thrown herself at their poor, unsuspecting boy. They packed up her things, dropped her off at a home for troubled girls and never looked back.

The first few nights in the home Dorothy cried herself to sleep. Life had been so simple in Oz, and there were people there who loved her. She had to find some way to get back, but without the slippers she just didn't know how.

As the time passed and Dorothy's belly grew, she got more and more attached to the little human inside of her. She'd never been around pregnant women before, but the home was full of them. Even though they were all going through the same thing, they shunned Dorothy because of her crazy talk about witches and talking scarecrows.

Dorothy seemed to have the most active child in her womb, constantly kicking away at her insides. At first it was annoying, no other girl had such an active baby, but as the months went by she took it as a sign of communication with her child. She would spend the day reminiscing about Oz and the fetus would kick in response. With her due date approaching, she was glad the kicking would soon stop, though.

Her dreams of Oz and delivering the baby there had started a few weeks before. They were mostly all the same—Glenda and her loving ways guiding the baby out of Dorothy while she was surrounded by all her friends. She was sure the dreams meant something, but she didn't know what.

That night she lay in bed wishing for a different life. How had things spun out of control so quickly? These thoughts were swirling around in her head when she drifted off to sleep.

The dream started out the way it always did. There Glenda sat at the foot of her bed between Dorothy's legs. This time Glenda wasn't telling her to push. She looked calm and smiled warmly at Dorothy. Was this real?

"Oh, Glenda!" cried Dorothy. "I miss Oz. I want to come back. My life is such a mess!"

"My sweet child," Glenda replied. "We all walk a certain path, a predetermined destiny, and you are on the right track."

"But how?' Dorothy asked. "How can the mess I've made of my life be the right path?"

"There are signs everywhere. You must open your eyes dear. Every small event is meant to kick you in the right direction," Glenda explained. "You will truly find your home once you realize what's inside of you. You now have the power to come home."

Dorothy's eyes shot open, and she sat up with a start. She understood what Glenda was telling her.

"Kick!" she screamed.

Dorothy looked down to her bun in the oven and realized the baby wasn't kicking at all! It was clicking! She was feeling the clicking of the baby's heels. She rubbed her tummy.

Dorothy closed her eyes. She didn't need the slippers after all. Home was only three heel clicks away. The power and will inside her was ultimately all that she needed to return to the Promised Land.

"There's no place like home!" she cried as her belly gave her a jolt. She repeated the phrase with the same result. She took in a deep breath and squeezed her eyes tight, saying it one final time as her baby's heels clicked together for the third time.

Dorothy opened her eyes and was greeted by the warm smile she saw so vividly in her dreams. Dorothy smiled in return. This time she could hear her as clear as day.

"Welcome home, Dorothy."

About the Author

Traci Lewis was born, raised, and still lives in Small Town, Arkansas. This is her first publication, and she is over-the-moon to be published with such talented authors. For the last year, Traci has been Yard Dog Press's little bitch, following every demand of their fearless leader, Selina Rosen, and enjoying every minute of it.

Traci has been involved in Community Theater the past several years and jumps at the chance to be on stage. She enjoys most every sport and is an avid video game player. Traci is grateful for this opportunity and looks forward to continuing her writing.

Not in Kansas Anymore

Rhonda Eudaly

"Here we go." Dorothy slammed her foot down on the accelerator of the storm chasing vehicle—the TorChasinator 5000, slinging the steering wheel to the left, throwing her crew against their harnesses. The warning came too late.

"But..." The girl's voice sounded young. "I don't think we're in Kansas anymore."

Dorothy slammed her foot on the brakes. "What did I say I'd do if I heard anyone in this crew say that? *What. DID. I. SAY?*"

"She's new, Boss. She didn't know!" Cal, the trendily scruffy man in the co-pilot seat, said. "You can't do that. That's an F3 out there."

"She's had fair warning, Cal, just like everyone else." Dorothy clutched the wheel, white-knuckled. "She's out. Now."

"I just meant we passed the state line. We've passed into Oklahoma. I saw the sign!" The girl sputtered in panicked confusion.

"You're not putting anyone out of this vehicle in the middle of a chase. I won't let you." Dorothy and Cal traded glares, electricity all but sparking between them. "We're a team. We stay together."

Dorothy broke eye contact with the man and jerked her head toward the girl. "Teach her, Cal. This one's on you. Because next time...it can be an F5 for all I care...she's out." Dorothy hit the gas again. "Now everyone hang on."

Wizard, the seemingly mind-reading bartender, already had Dorothy's drink on the bar when she shoved through the door of the only bar in 20 miles. "No luck?"

Dorothy growled as she took the drink and stomped over to "her" table in the far corner. The rest of the TorChasinator 5000 crew gathered up their drinks and spread out through the bar. They weren't the only patrons, but their arrival did seem to double the population.

"What's with Toto?" Wizard nodded toward the new girl perched on a stool at the end of the bar staring into her drink.

Cal took a hit off his soft drink—someone had to be able to

drive the chase vehicle on a moment's notice—and tried not to snort. All members of the TorChasinator's crew were "TOTO" until Dorothy decided to learn their names. Cal knew them all. He'd been with Dorothy since the beginning of her storm chasing days, which had been before storm chasing was cool.

"Why would she *act* like that?" Toto nearly wept into her drink and didn't seem to be speaking to anyone in particular.

Cal sighed and exchanged a look with the bartender. "Time for *The Talk*, Wizard?"

He nodded. No one knew his real name. Everyone called him Wizard, and he never corrected them. "Let's see what happens when the house falls on this one."

Cal went over to the girl. "Come on, Toto. It's time."

"Time for what?" the girl asked. "And why does everyone keep calling me Toto?"

"I'm about to explain that to you."

Dorothy sat nursing her drink. "Munchkins." It sounded like a curse word.

"You know you said that out loud, right?"

Her head snapped up, a scathing remark on the verge of shooting out. Only because it was Wizard kept her from unleashing her wrath. He raised an eyebrow at her as he pulled out the chair across from her and plopped down.

"Talk."

"We were so close. I could feel it," Dorothy said.

"What was it?"

"F3."

"That doesn't seem strong enough, and that's not what I meant." Wizard sighed and leaned forward. "How long have we known each other?"

"Too long."

"Then what was it?"

"Toto. She said The Thing. She knew the rules."

"You didn't ditch her."

"Cal wouldn't let me. I wanted to. She would've been okay."

"Not everyone is as nearly immortal as you."

"Munchkins." There was the curse word again. "I didn't ask for this, you know."

"I know. Are you *sure* you're going about this is the best way?"

"*BEST*? I have no idea. It's better than sitting around waiting for a twister to find me. At least I'm making a living now, thanks to cable television networks. Not like when I was...younger."

"But is it worth risking—or losing—crew members?"

Dorothy tossed back the rest of her drink. "No one in the TorChasinator crew has died on my watch."

"Not yet. You're not the most cautious person."

"Caution kills people in this line of work."

"*Line of work*? You make it sound like some career path—like accounting. It's not. It's not a holy calling either. It's not even a real *job*."

"Says the bartender."

"Tell me, Dorothy, is it worth it? Is getting back to Oz *really* that important? How many years...how many *decades* have you been trying? And what has it gotten you?"

"Not rich, that's for sure. Everyone else has made out like bandits on my story but me. I knew I shouldn't have trusted that Baum guy, or those movie guys. And don't get me started on Auntie Em, and her crappy money management. But I'm not bitter."

"Of course not. Why would you be?"

She shot him a dirty look. "Sarcasm? Really?"

"*NO WAY!*"

The incredulous outburst drowned out all conversations for a second as all heads shot toward the sound. Dorothy shrugged. "Guess Cal told Toto."

Tornado sirens screamed to life as across the bar, phone alarms blared. Dorothy and her crew were on their feet and halfway to the door before the first notes faded away. Dorothy glanced back at Wizard. "Wish us luck?"

She was gone before he could respond. She didn't do much more than scan the crew as they piled into the TorChasinator. The new girl was the last one. Dorothy stopped her. "You with us, Toto?"

The girl grinned wildly. "All the way."

Her response threw Dorothy for a moment. "You're sure?"

"If even half—or heck, less—of what Cal told me is true, I want in. All the way. All the way to Oz."

"Oh, Sweetie, if you're looking for the Judy Garland, Frank Baum versions, you're going to be in for a rude awakening."

"Were there really flying monkeys?"

"Oh, yes."

"'Nuf said. Let's go."

"We have to go *now* or we'll lose the storm!" Cal yelled from the cab.

Dorothy pushed the girl in ahead of her. Cal sealed the vehicle's doors behind them as they all took their positions. Dorothy floored the accelerator and shot out of the parking lot. She looked over at the new girl. "What's your name, Toto?"

"Glenda."

"Of course it is. Now, find me that storm."

The TorChasinator sat momentarily idle in the parking lot of an abandoned cinderblock gas station. Wind whipped around them, kicking up dirt, debris, and other bits.

"Holy cow," Cal said. "Is that what I think it is?"

Dorothy couldn't hide her glee. "That's our ticket. That's the buildup to an F5, and we're going into the heart of it. Anyone thinking I wasn't serious about any of this—that it was all talk—well, here's the reckoning. I'm going in. I'm going back to Oz."

"You're serious?" one of the older crew members said. "You're seriously going to drive into the heart of that thing?"

Dorothy turned to face the computer tech who monitored the weather sensors. He'd been with the crew for several years. She felt torn between rage and disappointment. "You've been with me long enough to know I don't bluff like that and I've never, *ever*, hidden my intentions."

"But...but...that's a story! Not real!"

"Then I suggest you shelter here. The building's sturdy. You'll be okay." Dorothy looked around at her crew. "Anyone else?"

Dorothy drove into the storm with only Cal and Glenda. The rest stayed behind.

"Hang on; it's about to get bumpy."

Dorothy hit the gas and sped straight for the giant funnel just starting to eat its way across the Kansas countryside. The closer they came, the more it seemed like the tornado tried to escape them, but Dorothy didn't let it get away. In a split second, they were in the heart of the twister.

"Hit it, Cal. Now!"

Cal reached over to a panel and almost hit the giant red button—the one *no one* was *ever* supposed to touch lest they unleash the End of the World. "Really?"

"NOW!"

Cal slapped his palm down on the red button with a six-year-old's glee. The cabin immediately was bathed in an eerie light.

"There's no place..."

"*Do. NOT. FINISH. THAT. SENTENCE!!!*"

Glenda gulped and bit her lips closed as Dorothy threw the TorChasinator into an overdrive never dreamed of by the original manufacturer. The vehicle spun, twisted, and bucked in ways carnival ride creators only dreamed off. Then, before they knew it, it was over. The TorChasinator came to a bumpy landing on solid ground once more.

The remaining three TorChasinator crew stood outside the vehicle staring around at the rural landscape. The foliage was thicker and more vibrantly colored than anything Cal or Glenda had ever experienced. Dorothy seemed to be reacting like seeing an old friend.

"One of you can say it now," Dorothy said.

"*REALLY?*" Cal didn't bother hiding the surprise in his voice. "Seriously?"

"Yeah. This once. Because we're so not."

"We're not what?" Glenda asked, not following the conversation for all the distractions around.

Cal, however, met Dorothy's grin with a wide, incredulous one of his own. "We're not in Kansas anymore."

"Welcome to Oz," Dorothy said. "Though it's different than I remember. Wilder."

"Well, it has been a while," Cal said. "That would make sense."

A roar in the trees snapped their attention to their surroundings.

"Was that what I think...?" Cal asked.

"Lion!" Dorothy's whole face lit up and she started toward the trees.

Cal stopped her. "Wait. If you think things are different, do you really want to go charging off like that?"

Dorothy stopped short, confused and considering Cal's words. "Okay, new plan. We're going to see the wisest...person...I know here."

"Where are we going?" Glenda asked as Dorothy shooed them back into the TorChasinator.

"The Emerald City."

"But according to the story, the Wizard left Oz before you did."

"I never said we were going to see the Wizard." Dorothy sealed the door behind them. "At least we don't have to walk this time. Let's roll."

"But how do we get there?" Cal asked. "It's not like it's in the GPS."

"That's where you'd be wrong." Dorothy pulled a program up on the computer and fed it into the navigation system. "How carefully did you look around, Cal?"

"Apparently not carefully enough. What did I miss?"

"Check the turf out there about three o'clock. Tell me what you see in the grass."

Cal leaned forward and squinted through the Plexiglas windshield. "Is that yellow rock out there?"

"Brick, actually. I spent years programming the sensors to detect the yellow brick. We can follow the road all the way in, visible or not."

"I thought the Emerald City was supposed to be green," Cal said with a note of disappointment as the TorChasinator crew found themselves being escorted through the white stone streets. "How come it's not?"

"The Scarecrow must've done away with the green glasses." Dorothy shuddered. "Good riddance. They were...awful."

Within moments they were led to the palace in the center of town, leaving Dorothy with a major case of déjà vu. The Scarecrow met them in the waiting room but stopped short.

"Who are you?" he asked.

Dorothy couldn't hold back. In a rare public display of affection, she threw her arms around the Scarecrow and squeezed the stuffing out of him. "I've missed you most of all, Scarecrow!"

The Scarecrow gently but firmly pushed her away. "Again I say, *Who are you*?"

"It's me, Dorothy."

"Dorothy is but a young girl. You're...not. And it hasn't been that long. Only a few years."

"What? No!" Dorothy swayed on her feet. "What have those evil Munchkins done to me now? I swear, Scarecrow, it's me. I'll prove it to you."

She leaned in close to his painted ears and whispered into his stuffing. He drew back—being unable to widen his eyes or blush. "*Dorothy*! It *is* you! You've come back to us! I take it the temporal stream moves differently in your Kansas reality than it does here."

"I suppose so. But we have all the time in the world to catch up, now. Are the Tin Woodsman and the Lion still with us?"

"Indeed. They'll be delighted to know you're back. But surely you want to get back to Kansas. That's all you wanted when you were here last."

"Let's just say Kansas has lost its appeal. And before you ask, the crazy shoes only worked one way."

"It's not the only reason you've returned," Glenda said, her voice sounding...different.

All eyes turned to her as her skin started to glow white hot and shimmer. Suddenly, she wasn't Glenda, the young, naïve storm chaser. She became...more. The Scarecrow backed away from her and Dorothy. "The Witch! The Good Witch has returned!"

"You've *got* to be kidding me," Cal said. "Really?"

"We had to make sure you were ready to return. To fulfill your destiny," Glenda said.

Dorothy put both fists on her hips. "My only destiny is to find whatever Munchkin made me outlive everyone I've ever cared about and kick some tiny butt."

"No. You're not." Glenda looked past them. "I think they're ready. She has the spark necessary."

"Who're you talking to?" Cal asked.

"Pay no attention to the man behind the curtain," another, familiar voice said as Wizard the Bartender stepped out from behind the throne.

Dorothy and Cal stared at him and at each other in dumbfounded shock. Dorothy recovered first as she launched herself toward him. "You knew all along!? You let me struggle all those years. All those *decades*, trying to get back when you had the way all along?"

"You needed to find your own way. So did Cal."

"Wait. What? What do I have to do with any of this?" Cal asked, still stunned. "I just came along for the ride."

"No, it was much more than that." Wizard looked at Glenda. "Are you thinking what I'm thinking?"

"She's perfect for the West. He'll be good in the East. They balance each other."

"Are you saying I look like a house fell on me?" Cal asked.

"Are you saying I'm some kind of Wicked Witch?" Dorothy demanded. "Newsflash, I don't melt when I get wet."

"Of course not—to both of you. You will help balance Oz's

power once more."

"Is this one of those 'You kill it. You become it.' Stories? 'Cuz those have been done to death."

"No. You were always meant to be here. You just helped your way along the first time."

"What about me?" Cal asked.

"Your family has always been tied to Oz, Cal. You just never knew it." Wizard shimmered and changed shape.

"Dad?! You...you disappeared...What? Why?"

Glenda gestured with her magically reappearing wand. "Come. We'll explain it all."

Dorothy stood on the balcony of the castle she once feared and looked out across the Western horizon. With a little time and some ingenuity, she could make it more comfortable. It had been an incredible two weeks since she'd returned to Oz. And where she once looked on the talking mice and flying monkeys as magic, she knew better now.

There was no great desert between Oz and Kansas. The Munchkins didn't actually curse her. And the talking field mice never shut up. She loved it all. Even finding out her childhood magic was really a great alien genetic experiment. Like a terrarium, only cooler and much more important.

"The calibrations are finished on the dimensional bubble," Cal said, coming up behind her, wiping grease off his hands. "I don't think that thing's been maintained since you offed the last Witch of the West."

"I wouldn't doubt it. Thanks, Cal."

"You know you're going to have to learn to do maintenance and repairs on your own, right?"

"I know. I know. But I'm still adjusting, and you're a familiar face. You heading East soon?"

Cal nodded. "Yeah, I have some housekeeping to do there as well. This is trippy, isn't it?"

Dorothy smiled. "Trippy doesn't even cover it. Be careful of the flying monkeys. Nice creatures, but they leave terrible messes."

"Got it. You going to be okay?"

"You bet. Haven't you heard, I'm the Wicked Witch of the Wild, Wild West. What's not to love?"

"You don't have to be wicked, or mix your pop culture references, you know."

"You're taking all the fun out of it." Dorothy pretended to pout. "Besides, there are several definitions of *wicked*."

"I really do need to get back East before the Munchkins redecorate for me. No one wants that. I understand you better, now."

Dorothy laughed. "Why do you think I didn't fight the Western Assignment? Come on, I'll give you a ride back. Can't have you risking sleeping forever in the poppy field."

"You're on."

The TorChasinator tore across Oz, antennae waving in the breeze, at full speed, bouncing across the terrain in carefree abandon as if it, too, had found its way home.

About the Author

Rhonda Eudaly lives in Arlington, Texas with her husband and two dogs. She's worked in various industries to support her writing career. She loves music, writing, and is watching her smiley face collection being overtaken by rubber ducks of all shapes and sizes. Rhonda Eudaly's work is featured in *The Four Redheads of the Apocalypse*; *Redheads of the Apocalypse: Apocalypse Now*; *Flush Fiction*; *International House of Bubbas*; *A Bubba in Time Saves None*; *More Stories That Won't Make Your Parents Hurl*; and many others. Check out her website - www.RhondaEudaly.com - for the links and more information.

Even Black is Bright in Oz
Trina Jacobs

"Now we can stay in Oz forever!" said Toto, as he and Dorothy watched the Wizard fly away without them. She didn't hear him, people rarely did. His whole body wagged as he licked her face. Her tears were deliciously salty.

Not long after the Wizard left, Dorothy scooped Toto up and they whirled through the air, then tumbled to a stop in a barren field. Dorothy lost her shoes, though she didn't seem to care. Everything was gray. Even the air smelled gray. "How did we get back to Kansas?" asked Toto, "I thought we were staying in Oz."

A grin spread across Dorothy's face. "Toto, we're home!" As she ran toward the farmhouse, she shouted, "Aunt Em! Uncle Henry! I'm home!" Toto was happy because his girl was happy, so he ran with her, barking greetings to those they'd left behind.

Aunt Em hurried out to the porch, still wiping her hands on a dishtowel. Dorothy ran straight to her and pulled her close in a hug. The bony gray woman stiffened, then put her hands on the girl's shoulders and held her an arm's length away. She scowled at Dorothy. "Where have you been?"

"The cyclone blew me and Toto to Oz—"

Aunt Em snorted. "I don't care to listen to your lies. Just wait until your uncle comes in."

"I'm sorry ma'am," said Dorothy. Toto tried to convince her to hide under the bed with him.

Uncle Henry started in on Dorothy the moment he came in the door. He glared at her and she flinched from his gaze. He smelled angry. Toto curled himself into a tighter ball and tucked his tail even further between his legs.

"I didn't mean to leave," whispered Dorothy.

Uncle Henry pounded his fist on the table. "You took the damn house! I had to build a new one because of you! Not to mention replacing the stove and building new furniture. Do you see any trees around here? Do you know what wood costs?"

I guess we were supposed to bring the house back, thought Toto.

Dorothy squeaked, "I'm sorry."

"Why didn't I stay in Oz?" asked Dorothy as she fell into bed that night.

"I wondered that, too," said Toto, "so did the Straw Man." She held him close and he licked her tears away again.

"We'll go back to Oz," said Toto. Dorothy wiped at her tears with a corner of the bed sheet. "We'll bring everybody this time."

The little black dog yawned and closed his eyes. He dreamed that he was back in Oz. His tail wagged and he made happy noises in his sleep. Bright colors surrounded him; not even the shadows were dull. Best of all, Dorothy was happy.

The next morning Toto charged into the barn. "What are you so excited about?" asked the oldest milk cow. She was a Kansas cow, dull in mind and body. Her coat was a light grayish color with darker grayish spots.

"Listen, everybody!" said Toto. Ears flicked his way and the gray chickens kept on being chickens. He didn't expect them to listen anyway. "We're going to Oz!"

The gray horse pricked his ears and said, "What's an 'Oz?'"

Toto laughed. "It's a wonderful place with new smells and colors!"

"Colors?" asked a cow. If she'd had an eyebrow, she would have raised it. "What are colors?"

Toto danced in circles, his eyes bright. "We don't have them here. They're dazzling and happy, and they're in Oz – that's where me and Dorothy went."

Another cow, also gray with gray spots, said, "I thought a cyclone blew you away."

Toto grinned at her. "Nope. We took the house and went to Oz."

Even the chickens were quiet.

"I talked to Dorothy about it last night. I told her we should all go this time."

"And she understood you?" said the oldest cow.

"I'm sure she did!" said Toto as he sprinted from the barn.

Every morning, noon, and night for two whole days Toto asked Dorothy when they were going back to Oz. She never answered, but she cried a lot.

While supervising the chickens one day, Toto thought, *What if*

Dorothy doesn't know how to get back to Oz? He ignored his charges as the idea swirled around in his head.

"Kansas is grey and has no magic," he said to himself. "Oz has color and magic." He stood and cocked his head to the left and then to the right. "I can't see any color here, but it's everywhere in Oz. I can't find magic here either, but I didn't even have to look for it in Oz." Toto pondered for a moment, then pricked his ears and barked, "Color is magic! Magic is color!" He ran around the yard scattering the chickens and irritating the cows.

"Are we going to Oz now?" asked one of the cows. "You're stirring up enough dust to make a cyclone."

"Soon!" said Toto.

Dorothy watched the little dog spin joyous circles around her. "I'll find the magic for you!" he said, "then we'll go back to Oz!" She smiled, just a bit, for the first time in days.

Toto sniffed everywhere. He dug up flowers and patches of grass, but no colors hid there. There wasn't any magic behind the stove, under the covers, or on the highest shelf. He checked under chickens and inside of eggs, but he couldn't find it anywhere.

The next day, while Toto was helping Uncle Henry and the gray horse plow, a scent stopped him in his tracks. It wasn't a Kansas smell. He breathed in the co-mingled scents of Oz, magic, leather, and Dorothy. His tail wagged frantically as he dug into the newly turned earth. He uncovered Dorothy's silver shoes. They glistened like nothing from Kansas ever could. He stared at them in wonder as he breathed in their beautiful scent, then he grabbed them and ran to find Dorothy.

He never made it.

As he ran, Toto thought about the Land of Oz and the Emerald City. He slid to a stop on a yellow brick road and stared around in amazement. He was in the Emerald City. His jaw dropped open and the silver shoes fell to the ground. The capital of Oz wasn't brilliant green anymore; it was full of wondrous colors. Toto looked down at his paws. They were still black, but it was Oz black, not Kansas black.

People came out of shops and houses and hurried over to him. "Welcome back, Toto!" they said. The women curtsied and the men bowed. Everyone smiled at him. "You look well," said a young man. A woman asked after Dorothy, and several others chimed in. "Is she well? Is she coming back soon?"

The Straw Man came running when he spotted the little dog in the center of the ecstatic crowd. "How delightful to see you again, Toto!" he said. He searched the crowd and his burlap brow furrowed. "Didn't Dorothy come with you?"

Toto jumped into his arms. "I didn't mean to leave her behind!" he said, and then explained what happened.

The Straw Man lifted his hat and scratched his head. "I'll think of a way to bring Dorothy back to Oz."

"Great!" said Toto. "I told everybody they could come." He thought for a moment. "Though we might want to leave Uncle Henry and Aunt Em behind."

About the Author

Trina Jacobs was born on Halloween. Her friends say that explains a lot.

She left her hometown, Oswego, NY, after college, when she realized that there are places where winter lasts less than six months. She moved to Oklahoma, where she followed her dream of training horses and teaching riding lessons for several years before deciding that a steady paycheck might be nice.

Her work has appeared in *Trail Rider Magazine, Trail Blazer, Big Pulp, The Drabbler, The Daily Flash 2011,* and *Alpha Centauri*. She is working on her first novel, an urban fantasy about vampires and werewolves and witches (oh my!)

Trina lives near Tulsa, OK with her husband, one horse, one dog, and three cats.

Silver Slippers

vickey malone kennedy (vck)

A gray stiletto flew through the window crashing into the back of the gardener's head with a loud clang. He had learned from hard experience that shoes fly so he had fashioned himself a hat, wiring tin pie pans together, to form a protective shield from hurling footwear. He bent over to retrieve the discarded pump just as its mate was propelled through the air. The second shoe hit him squarely in the seat of his soil stained pants.

"Those are not the shoes I want," a voice shrilled from the other side of the window.

Miss Dottie had earned the title of "Eccentric Old Lady." Having come into a small fortune of her own as a very young girl and then later marrying a wealthy man, she was financially well off enough to be called "eccentric" instead of insane. Still, there were plenty of folks that called her "just plain crazy."

"Now, now, Gran-ma-ma," John said. "We've been through this a thousand times. There are no silver slippers in this house. As far as I know there never have been any silver slippers in this house. It's just an old fairytale. You're confused."

"I'm no more confused than you, you brainless boy. You think because you're young you know everything and because I'm old I don't know anything. Well let me tell you young man, I have forgotten more than you will ever learn."

She paused forgetting what she was shouting about for a moment. "One thing I know for certain is that there is a pair of silver — not boring old gray — slippers stashed away somewhere in this house and by golly I want them found."

"Whatever for, Gran-ma-ma?"

"I need them to get back."

"Get back? Get back to where?"

Miss Dottie's eyes clouded over as if she might cry. She knew where she wanted to go, she just didn't know if it was actually a real place. The Emerald City was such a faded memory she could no longer be certain it ever existed — except in her dreams.

She had told her children all about her wonderful childhood adventures. But she had grown up, leaving childhood things behind, long before her youngest grandson John was born. She had never told him about the wonderful wizard or the talking scarecrow when he was a boy. Now he stared at her as if he mistook her reminiscing for the ravings of a demented old woman.

Surely his father had told him the tales. Then again, perhaps not. Her own children had never really believed her stories. They often told her they thought them nothing more than delightful fables fabricated by her for their enjoyment.

Miss Dottie missed her children. They were grown and had children of their own and rarely visited except on holidays or when they wanted money. Money, of course, was the reason for John's visit. He had been to a fancy boarding school in France and was determined to become an artist with Miss Dottie as his benefactor.

"I'll tell you all about the Emerald City and you can draw pictures of it for me," she said temporarily distracted from her search.

Lately she spent most of her time searching for those shoes. She was certain she had stored them away, out of reach of her children when they were young, and had forgotten where she had hidden them. From time to time some random memory, stirred by a distant crow's caw, would inspire a new search.

When her oldest granddaughter was born she searched for days thinking that someday Jenny should have the slippers. She had never considered passing them along to her own children. By the third granddaughter she realized that it would be unfair for only one girl to have them and these girls were not raised to share.

Lately — the last dozen years or so — she would catch a glimpse of emerald green in the distance over the dull gray Kansas fields and be reminded of the silver slippers and the journey they had taken her on when she was a girl. She would be reminded of the friends she had not entirely forgotten; though they had faded into the shadows of her memory so deeply she could hardly conjure them up without some outside reminder.

From time to time the sun glistened off the gardener's pie pan hat, when he tilted his head in just such a fashion, and she would be reminded of a woodman built entirely of metal standing stiffly in the midst of a great forest. The woodman would never have felt comfortable in her meager gardens surrounded by treeless gray fields.

But still she could almost see him there.

From time to time she would catch a glimpse of the sparkle of gold flashing down the dirt road leading to the old homestead and be reminded of the yellow brick road she had traveled as a child. She would remember skipping along arm and arm with the talking scarecrow listening to him go on and on about brainless matters. She would giggle aloud to herself ignoring the questioning stares of those who whispered "she's lost her mind".

From time to time she would be awakened late at night, by the screech of an owl or the rustle of a branch against her bedroom window and, filled with a deep sense of fear and dread, be reminded of the knocking knees of a dear old friend that would have been more frightened than she by those scary sounds. It was so much easier for her to be brave about being all alone in her big empty house whenever she thought of the lion whose roar was bigger than his bite. Her memories of his bravery in the face of his fears made it easier for her to face her own.

Whenever she was reminded of the Emerald City, or the friends she had left behind, she would remember the silver slippers and the search would be on again. The search for the silver slippers always led to flying footwear, scampering servants and fidgety family. She knew everyone doubted her mental stability. Indeed she doubted it herself from time to time.

"Oh, please, Gran-ma-ma. It would be such a dull drawing; everything green. Besides I'm really not interested in those ridiculous stories. I came here to discuss an important matter."

"Important matter?"

For a moment she couldn't recall what his important matter was about nor could she recall what she had been looking for. It was important. Of that she was certain. But what? She could not recall.

"Just how much is this important matter of yours going to cost me?" she asked.

"Don't be so cynical, Gran-ma-ma."

"Don't call me cynical and then expect me to write you a check, you silly boy."

John bit his bottom lip. If he could have his way he'd no doubt have her declared incompetent and placed in a Nursing Home. She knew his father, uncles and cousins would never agree to such a thing. Not that they came around often enough to know her current condition.

It wasn't that they didn't care. It was more that she had made them feel unwelcomed. She became bored with them easily, shooing them away quickly, or urged them not to come at all. Of course there was also the eminent threat of shoe bombing that kept most visitors at bay.

Still she regretted not seeing her children more often. If they had half a brain among them they would know she really wanted them to come, even though she seldom enjoyed their company. They rarely ventured this far out into the Kansas countryside unless they wanted something from her. They never seemed to appreciate what she wanted to give them.

Oh yes, the slippers. She had been searching for the slippers. Perhaps Jenny would want them after all. No. She was much too old for the slippers now. All grown up and expecting a child of her own, Jenny was much too old to appreciate the slippers.

"Oh stop pouting, John," she said. "Have Agnes bring some tea to the garden and tell me all about these sketches of yours."

Miss Dottie greeted the gardener at the patio door. He nodded, smiled politely and handed her the gray heels.

"Good heavens Nathan, where did these come from?" she asked.

"The window ma'am."

"How odd," she said.

"Oh no ma'am," he responded. "Flying shoes are not the least bit odd around here."

"They're perfectly gaudy. No one could possibly walk in these things. Burn them."

"Of course ma'am."

Nathan turned to hand the shoes to Agnes after she placed the tea set on the patio table. A dented metal trash can lid belted to the back of his pants clattered and rattled as he walked away.

"Nathan," Miss Dottie squealed. "What are you doing with that ridiculous lid tied to your bottom?"

"Just guarding my flank, Miss Dottie," he said tipping his pie pan hat in her direction.

Agnes dusted off the gray shoes and scurried off toward the shoe closet.

John babbled on about studying in France, the museums he had visited and his sudden desire to become a painter. Paint chips fluttered from beneath the eaves of the patio cover and around the shutters. Perhaps John would like to paint them for her. Perhaps he could paint the entire house a nice cornflower blue. She had once visited a lovely place where all the houses were painted blue.

She grew weary of John's babbling. There was a time when a young man's babbling could hold her attention. Well, not actually a man, rather the man stuffed with straw. He had a tendency to babble on and on because he could not organize his thoughts well enough to express them without babbling.

"For goodness sake, John. Is your head filled with straw? Do you have a clue what you're talking about?"

John stared at her for a long moment then his eyes darkened with anger and his face flushed bright red. "The question is, Gran-ma-ma, do you have a clue what anyone is talking about?"

"Usually money. My money. Spending my money. Isn't that what you were talking about, John, dear?"

He gulped hard.

Miss Dottie sipped her tea peeking over the top of John's head toward the old dirt road. A dark shadow trotted across the hillside reminding her of a little black dog she had once known. She had given up pets after John's father was born. The poor boy was allergic to all animals. So, like any good mother, she had given up that which brought her joy for the sake of her child. A child that hadn't visited in over a year.

"Toto?"

"What is it, Gran-ma-ma?"

"A little black dog," she answered. "There. Across the field. Did you see him?"

John looked over his shoulder. "There isn't any dog there, Gran-ma-ma." He turned back to her with a deep scowl on his face. "Maybe you should have your vision checked."

"Nothing wrong with my vision boy," she said. "But somehow I've managed to surround myself with blind people."

He stared blankly at her as if he didn't understand a word she muttered. John wasn't a slow boy; not really, he just wasn't nearly as bright as he obviously thought himself to be. He shook his head, no doubt convinced she had truly lost what little was left of her mind. At least he had enough sense not to say it aloud. He sipped his tea with a muddled expression on his face. She wondered if he was plotting a way to convince the family that she needed to be put away somewhere for her own safety.

"I think it's passed my nap time," she said. "You run along now

John and let me sleep on this artsy-fartsy plan of yours. I just might be interested in financing this tom foolery. Besides, I wouldn't mind going to France. I think I'll take a few art classes myself."

John spilled tea onto his lap. He jumped up dropping the fragile cup and saucer onto the patio. They shattered into pieces. Tiny shards of green china splattered across the concrete creating dancing rainbows of light.

His eyes were filled with the feared anticipation of a severe scolding. Of course it was her right as a senile old lady to behave exactly the opposite of the way people expected. Instead of scolding him she clapped her hands together, like a delighted child, enjoying the green prisms' streaming reflections.

"Oh, how beautiful," she said.

"Very well, Gran-ma-ma, you get some rest and I'll return tomorrow. I really must have an answer as soon as possible. There are arrangements to be made and I should very much like to visit my parents for a few days before returning abroad."

"You've spent too much time abroad, if you ask me," she said. "You've become a bit uppity in your youth, Johnny."

He frowned. She knew how much he hated being called Johnny. He took her elbow helping her back into the house toward the stairs. She felt so frail next to the strapping young man. At the foot of the stairs she turned and patted his cheek.

"You shouldn't worry so much, Johnny. You'll get wrinkles. Your face is already scrunched up so much one would think you had just dropped a house on someone."

"I worry about you Gran-ma-ma."

"You've always been such a sweet boy, Johnny."

"Rest well, Gran-ma-ma. I'll come for lunch tomorrow and we can finish our discussion."

"Very well," she said. "Give me a hug and then off with you my sweet boy."

He did as he was told, then hurried away as if he were anxious to escape from her.

Miss Dottie climbed the stairs slowly. Not because she was too tired to climb them any faster but because she had forgotten why she was headed up them in the first place. Surely she had some determined intention when she began the climb but it had slipped her mind before reaching the first landing. Oh well, it must not have been important. Perhaps she would remember after a nap.

She awoke to a low rumbling sound like the flapping of many wings upon the air and loud chattering and laughing noises. She sat straight up in the bed. The collar of her blue gingham night gown tightened around her neck like an unseen hand clutching at her throat through the darkness.

What would her dear friend the cowardly Lion do at a moment like this?

"Why he would roar very loudly until he drowned out the sounds of the night," she answered herself aloud.

The sound of her own voice startled her. It wasn't its usual dry rusty sound. There was an unexpected tinkling to it.

Miss Dottie sprang out of her bed and ran to the window. It was nearly dawn. Had she slept all afternoon and through the night?

A distant twinkling of gold glistening beneath the first streaks of pink painting the sky caught her attention. "Whatever could it be, Toto?"

She looked around searching for the little black dog – that had not been there for many years – half expecting to see him sitting at her feet, grinning up at her, wagging his tail. Perhaps the little black shadow darting out of her room was only a hallucination. Whatever it was Miss Dottie followed at a dangerously quick pace; much too fast for a woman of her age.

She took the stairs two at a time dashing out onto the dew drenched lawn in her stocking feet. The shadow bounced across the gray fields toward the sparkle of gold in the distance. Miss Dottie followed.

"Miss Dottie?" a frantic female voice called from inside the house.

She did not turn back. She raced across the field leaping, dancing and skipping like a child. She could make out the forms of yellow bricks creating a path toward the sunrise.

At the edge of the horizon she could see the shadowy outlines of a man stumbling toward her. He wobbled like one with legs made of straw. He was followed by a shiny man like one made of metal. And behind them, waiting patiently for her to come to him, stood the brave and loyal Lion.

Her heart pounded wildly in her chest threatening to burst through her sternum. A tight pressure around her ribs slowed her pace. She stumbled falling to her knees. Regaining her footing she ran faster than before. Her little feet, flying beneath her, barely touched the ground as she rushed toward the yellow brick road.

The voices behind her faded into the distance, as if they had suddenly stopped in mid chase and no longer followed her across the field.

"Call 9-1-1," Nathan yelled.

"No Nathan," answered Agnes. "It's too late. Let her go. She would want it that way."

Miss Dottie started to glance back to wave good-bye to Agnes and Nathan. A beautiful lady, dressed in a fancy sparkling white dress, suddenly materialized in front of her.

"Don't look back Dorothy," said Glenda. "You must never look back now dear."

"I shan't," she replied.

Then she saw the silver slippers, on a small gray mound, in the midst of the gray field. "However did they get out here so far away from the house?"

"They've always been here dear," replied Glenda the Good. "They've been waiting right here, where you left them, all these many years."

She slipped her feet into the slippers. They fit perfectly. She gasped when she saw her reflection in the toes of the shoes.

Her gingham nightgown had transformed into a crisply pressed gingham dress. Her stringy gray hair had grown into long dark waves. Even her face had changed. She was no longer the old lady that had struggled to climb the stairs. She was, once again, a lovely young girl.

She placed the toe of one silver slipper onto the first yellow brick of the road leading back to Oz. The Scarecrow threw a stuffed arm over her shoulder.

"Welcome home, Dorothy," he said guiding her along the road.

They skipped together until they met the Tin Woodman. Dorothy looped her arm through his sparkling metal arm. The three of them skipped toward the weeping Lion. Her beloved old friend held out his front paws waiting to embrace her.

About the Author

Originally from Alamo, Tennessee, vickey malone kennedy (aka **vck**—pronounced Vick) now lives in Oklahoma with her grown children, that man her children call daddy, three dogs, a ferret and her beautiful red-haired granddaughter, Miss Rhylee. **vck** is the winner of the 2011 Darrell Award for Best Midsouth Short Story for "Bobby Sue Almost Got Married" published by Yard Dog Press in the anthology "A Bubba In Time Saves None" and the winner of the coveted Oklahoma Writers' Federation Inc. 2011 Crème de la Crème award for her Western Novel "A Woman Alone". For more information about vck's writing and personal adventures visit her website www.vickeymalonekennedy.com

A Bad Case of the Munchies

Susan Satterfield

For the umpteenth time, Dorothy wished she'd never left Oz, even if the whole thing had only been a dream driven by tornado debris smashing her in the head. Hell, it would have been better if she'd never woken up at all. Both Auntie Em and Uncle Henry passed within two weeks of each other almost as soon as Dorothy graduated from high school, leaving Dorothy to deal with back taxes and a mortgage twice what the farm was actually worth. She'd sold off almost all the land leaving only the run down house and about an acre of weeds and stray chickens.

She'd sell that too if anyone would give her enough for it to get her the hell out of Kansas. *I should just put a 2 X 4 across my head. It'll either kill me, or send me back to Oz. Sounds like a win-win scenario.* Just as Dorothy was considering whether or not she was serious, a loud knock brought her back to reality. Not being in the mood for company, unless they were tall, handsome and carrying a butt load of cash, she was reluctant to go to the door.

Dorothy jerked open her front door, and found…nothing. She looked all around, but not a soul was there.

"Hey, toots! Down here. I'd appreciate it if you'd quit looking over me. Jeez. We never get any respect!"

Dorothy froze. The creature standing below her was small of stature, but clearly not short in attitude. It finally sank in that she was staring at a Munchkin, which should be impossible, but yet there he was…blue coat, striped leggings, pointy shoes and all. The only word she could utter was "…Munchkin."

"Great…you're not blind. What else would I be? We don't have time to waste. I'm Jaq. Glinda, the Good, sent me to fetch you right away, so let's go."

"G-g-go w-where?" Dorothy stuttered. She didn't feel like she had a knot on her head, so she didn't think she'd actually bashed in her own skull, but at this point anything was possible.

Jaq stared at her like she was an idiot, a concept she was starting to consider. Was she finally losing what little mind she had left? Clearly, that was the only answer left: she had to be stark raving mad.

"Oz, of course," Jaq snapped. Still, it was clear he was afraid of something, and trying hard not to show it. Finally, the strange little man just blurted it out. "We need your help. We don't know what to do, and even more frightening...Miss Glinda is as scared as we are. I've never seen her like this." Tears pooled in the corners of his emerald eyes. "Something strange is happening in Oz; something odd and very, very bad."

Grabbing Dorothy's hand, Jaq smacked his heels together three times repeating "There's no place like Oz" quickly, which didn't give Dorothy a chance to say yes, no, or go to hell. One second she was standing on her front porch, and the next she was standing, if you could call trying not to fall on her ass standing, in the private study of Glinda, the Good Witch from the South.

"It certainly took you long enough." Glinda's sweet voice couldn't sound really angry if she tried, but her eyes and body language clearly showed her irritation. "The Munchkin situation is getting worse."

Getting snapped at by a woman wearing a sparkly dress and crown was the last straw for Dorothy. "Okay. That's it. I've had it. First, Shorty over there pounds on my door jabbering about something bad, then the next thing I know I'm back in Oz standing in front of a figment of my imagination. Either wake me up or tell me what the hell is going on."

"Jaq didn't tell you what was going on?"

"Jaq didn't tell me diddley squat. He just showed up at my door, clicked his tiny heels together, and here we are. I don't know if I've gone completely off the deep end, or if this is really happening. Either way it's gotta be better than sitting in Kansas wondering what the hell to do with my life. Since I'm crazy anyway, exactly what is going on with the Munchkins?" Dorothy crossed her arms and stared defiantly at Jaq and Glinda. Jaq started to say something, but quickly decided against it when he caught the look in Glinda's eyes.

"Things have changed so much since you were last here. For a long time, everything went smoothly, but then about two months ago reports of strange occurrences began coming in from all parts of Oz. At first, I thought it was just a bad case of overactive imaginations, but that was before the first full attack." Glinda's pale skin seemed to grow even paler. "Munchkins are dying, and then coming back. However, what comes back is not the same. They become snarling, violent creatures attacking and...eating... anyone and anything getting in their way, " Glinda paused, her voice dropping to a whisper, "and that's not even the strangest part—those who are afflicted keep slowly repeating a single word over and over…brains—brains."

Dorothy burst out laughing. The only thing that had kept Dorothy from going completely insane was watching movies—old and new, so she knew it could only be one thing. "Zombies…you're telling me that Munchkins are becoming zombies."

"What's a zombie?" Glinda and Jaq asked at the same time.

"Zombies were once normal people who have been infected by a virus that kills them, but then brings them back as something neither dead nor alive. They are moving, always hungry, eating machines. Once they bite someone, then that person also dies and becomes a zombie. The only sure way to kill a zombie is either cut its head off entirely, or at least, destroy what's left of the brain—a bullet, a well-placed arrow. Of course, you could always blast them into pieces or burn them up, but you have to make sure they burn all the way up."

Glinda looked shocked, and Jaq appeared to be frozen in fear. Dorothy realized she had probably given them too much detail at one time. "But zombies aren't real."

Glinda let a little smile appear, which somehow almost made Dorothy feel better. "Dear, most people think we're not real, yet here we are." She sighed. "I'd hoped a simple magic spell would cure them, but for some reason my magic doesn't work on these…zombies. I'd hoped to save them."

"You can't save them. They're already dead. The only thing you can do is keep the contagion from spreading." Dorothy didn't like the idea of wandering around killing infected Munchkins any more than Glinda did, but she also knew it was the only way to insure the safety of everyone. "What's even more important is where did the first zombie come from? I mean there has to be a patient zero."

"The first attack was reported a week ago, and we've got about twenty munchkins zombies or whatever you call them quarantined near the closest border to Emerald City. There's another fifteen or so being held near the Eastern coast. It's not just this event. There've been reports of buildings, people, creatures- -all kinds of things— appearing and then disappearing. At first, it was chalked up to too much ale or even a strange illness. Then this happened."

Glinda's eyes became unfocused as if she was looking at something that wasn't there. Dorothy could tell she was concentrating almost too hard. Sweat popped up on her brow making her skin sparkle even more. "Oh, no…not here. I'm getting reports of some of the undead munchkin thingies near the Castle. I thought we'd gotten them all. I just don't have enough magic left to create another containment field. I'll need to recharge." She sighed.

Dorothy could see Glinda's hand trembling and could feel her underlying fear, and it did absolutely nothing for Dorothy's own confidence. Swallowing hard, Dorothy tried to sound tough. "Undead Munchkin thingies sounds almost cute. They're zombies. Glinda, you know what we have to do." Dorothy couldn't believe her own words. She was actually supporting the idea of destroying what had once been living creatures. "I don't suppose you have any guns."

"I don't keep weapons here. I'm a GOOD witch." Glinda seemed shocked Dorothy could even consider such a thing.

"Being good won't keep you from being eaten by a zombie Munchkin. We've got to stop them unless you just like the idea of Oz being taken over by flesh-eating zombies."

Glinda shook her head. "I know, I know, but is there no other way?"

"No one has to like it. We just have to do it, but how?"

"You said burning them would work?"

Dorothy shrugged. "If they're burned enough, I don't see why not."

"Fire bombs should do the trick." Glinda began frantically digging through drawers and cabinets. "I'd made a bunch up last week for the Festival of the Fairies. They should be here somewhere." A swirl of feathers, bits of tissue paper, and a few startled pixies floated in the air before coming to rest on any available surfaces. One dazed looking pixie landed on Dorothy's sleeve, but quickly darted away before she had a chance to even touch it.

"Here they are!" Glinda held up a delicately woven basket appearing filled with colorfully decorated eggs the Easter Bunny himself would've been proud of. "We should be able to use them to get rid of any zombies, or almost anything else for that matter, from a safe distance. It'll be messy, but if we hit them square, then there shouldn't be much more than ashes left." The usually happy face of the beautiful Good Witch displayed such pain it was hard not to suffer a broken heart right along with her. Someone so good, so perfect should never have to feel such pain. Glinda's graceful hand shook so much Dorothy reached over and took the trembling basket from her. If those eggs broke, Dorothy had the feeling an army of king's men wouldn't be able to find enough pieces to even attempt putting anything or anyone back together. Glinda grabbed Dorothy's free arm. "I can't believe this is the only option." Glinda's tear-filled eyes searched Dorothy's face for any sign, any glimpse of hope.

Wishing she had a different answer, Dorothy shook her head. "It's the only way." Glinda nodded, "Let's get this over with."

It didn't take long. There were only ten or twelve zombie munchkins, who exploded in a colorful display consisting of flame and smoke, leaving only a thin layer of pastel ash dusting the area. Once they knew how, it didn't take long to track down and erase the last of the little undead monsters.

Jaq was too exhausted to make a snide remark when Dorothy confronted Glinda. She still looked beautiful even though it was clear she was tired and more than a little emotional; even her golden locks hung limply as if they didn't have the strength to curl up properly. "What in the world is going on here? How did a Munchkin even come anywhere near a zombie, let alone close enough to get bitten?"

"That's just it," Glinda almost whispered. "I've got a feeling we haven't seen the last of the weirdness." She took a deep breath. "I know this sounds crazy, but I believe that somehow a parallel reality has somehow become "attached" to this one. While in this world magic works, and we use spells and magic shoes to travel between these realities, everything doesn't work the same in each reality." She gave a little smile. "Think about it Dorothy. Have you EVER heard of any place like Oz back in Kansas? That's because this place exists in an alternate reality to yours. To be honest, it was the great and powerful Oz himself who gave me that idea. He always did say I would have been a science fiction fan in your world."

"Too bad he wasn't a horror fan, then you would've known how to handle zombies."

Glinda laughed, "Why dear, that's why I sent Jaq after you. I remembered you being such a bright young lady when you were here last time. We needed someone who might know what those things were, and we were right—you knew just how to get rid of those things."

Dorothy smirked. "I guess having nothing to do but read every book in the library and watch every bad movie I could find on the four channels the TV did get came in handy. Although I'm still not sure it was worth being stuck for years in the middle of nowhere."

"Thank you, Dorothy. Once again Oz is in your debt. You aided in rescuing the Munchkins from a fate worse than death. The first time it was a wicked witch; this time it was a bunch of zombified munchkins. You've already done more than enough. Anytime you want to go home, Jaq will be glad to take you back."

Before Dorothy could even respond, the door to Glinda's study slammed open. A very distressed looking Winkie came rushing in almost babbling, "I can't. I mean, I must. I mean. Oh, no, I don't know what I mean." He fell to his knees and burst into yellow tears. "Miss Glinda—we-e-e need you. We-e-e do-o-n't know what to do." The Winkie was shaking so hard, Dorothy was afraid his pants would end up around his ankles

Glinda reached out and pulled the quivering Winkie back to his feet. "Dear, I can't help if you can't tell me what you need my help with." Dorothy could feel Glinda's magic at work as a calming wave of peace wrapped around everyone in the room. "Now dear, tell me your name and the problem you need help with."

With a huge sigh and golden streaks of tears marking his face, the Winkie looked straight into Glinda's caring eyes, "I'm Mick, ma'am. The Emperor sent me to you for help. We're being invaded by strange creatures we've never seen before!"

"What kind of creatures?" Dorothy and Glinda asked at the same time.

"Things like people who change into wolves and others who only inhabit the night and turn into a cloud of mist at the drop of a hat." Mick paused long enough to take another deep breath in an attempt to calm his shaken nerves. "That's not all, either. One of our scouts reported a giant lizard marching toward the Emerald City leaving a trail of destruction along the way." Mick's eyes filled with yellow tears once again. "Please Miss Glinda, we need your help!"

Glinda shot a pleading look at Dorothy who took a tiny moment to consider her options—she could stay in Kansas and go mad from boredom, or she could embrace the madness that was Oz.

Giving Glinda a quick hug, Dorothy turned to Jaq, "Come on Shorty! I'm going to need a gun, some silver bullets, a string of garlic, and a whole bunch of wooden stakes. The lizard I'll deal with later!" Dorothy had a feeling she was going to be in Oz for a very long time…and that was how it should be.

About the Author

Susan Satterfield is the author of a number of published short stories including "Mirror of His Soul" and "The Changing," appearing in *Eldritch Tales*, and "A Perfect World," appearing in the Yard Dog Press anthology, *Stories That Won't Make Your Parents Hurl*. Her chapbook, *Mirror Images*, was published by Yard Dog Press in May of 2002. "The Lady Killer" and "Sweet Teddy" appeared in an anthology entitled *Small Bites*, which was a benefit for author, Charles Grant. She is also the author of "A Bubba Poet" found in *The International House of Bubbas* and "What Goes Around" from the anthology *Flush Fiction*. Susan's short story entitled, "Close Encounters of the Bubba Kind," can be found in the Yard Dog Press anthology *Houston, We've Got Bubbas*. Her poem entitled "The Hunger: A Zombie Poem," appeared in October, 2009 in an anthology titled *Vicious Verses and Reanimated Rhyme* from Costcom Entertainment. She has a number of writing projects on (and sometimes under) the table.

Susan is an English Instructor at MCC- Longview in Lee's Summit, Missouri where she is founder and has been the coordinator for the MCC- Longview Literary Festival the past three years. She lives In Lee's Summit with her extended family including five dogs, two cats, and assorted fish.

It's A Dog's Life

Melyssa Childs-Wiley

The hissing and spitting as the Wicked Witch of the West melted was really rather disconcerting. After all, it is startling to see someone melt away to nothing to begin with, but I would have assumed that it would be a lot quieter than it really was. But there she was, talking about how she was going to melt, and then she proceeded to do so. I have to admit that the fact that she narrated her own death was admirable in its own way. Most people are so concerned with the fact that they were dying that they forget about the all-important dramatic narrative. I would have congratulated her on her creativity, but despite all of the other magical things that had happened on that very eventful trip, I did not manage to gain the ability to speak in a manner that humans would understand. I think that if we had stayed in Oz, though, I would have eventually learned how to do so.

You see, I'm a dog. Specifically, I'm a small, black, absolutely adorable, yet overwhelmingly modest, dog. I own a human girl whose name is Dorothy, and we went on an adventure together that no one here believes. Together we crossed the vast reaches, exploring new lands and killing Wicked Witches. We brought down the ruler of one land, and raised three new rulers to their Kingships. All as a result of Dorothy's quest to come home to Kansas. And then when we DID get home, she immediately told her Aunt Em and Uncle Henry everything that had happened.

She got it all wrong.

I understand why she would want to make herself the heroine of the story. It is probably embarrassing to admit that you would have been stuck there forever if you hadn't been saved by your dog more times than the dog has paws. But I really think that it was unreasonable of her to take ALL of the credit for things. I'm more than willing to share credit, even if all that she really did was hide behind the Cowardly Lion and cry for most of the trip.

Have you ever tried to hide behind a Cowardly Lion? It isn't easy. He is so busy running around looking for something that he can hide behind that it is hard to actually keep him between yourself and danger. It was impressive to see Dorothy manage it so often. Yes, I know that isn't how the story that you're familiar with goes. That's because Dorothy's version is the only one that anyone has ever heard.

The reality was very different.

It all started when the cyclone came. I was trying to drag Dorothy to the trap door to get into the storm cellar, but she was frozen with fear. Nothing I could do seemed to get through to her, and she just wouldn't move. When she finally did move toward the open door, it was too late, and the house was already in the air. Barking and snapping at her, I got her to hide under the bed where she would be safe. I pulled down a blanket and some pillows, and tucked her up into the corner while I stood guard until the house came down. We landed and went outside only to find out that the house had inadvertantly landed on a Witch, and not a very nice Witch at that. Things just went downhill from there.

A so-called Good Witch showed up but really wasn't any help at all. I tried to tell Dorothy that we shouldn't listen to these people, but she never seemed to get the message. Instead, she went along with what they said and began the quest to get to the Great and Powerful Oz. The next thing I knew, we were traipsing down that stupid road. Who makes yellow bricks anyway?

As she started gathering companions it got even crazier. Sure, they were some help in keeping her out of trouble, though it took a while for me to forgive the Lion for trying to eat me when all that I was doing was warning him off. But in the end they came in handy and had their uses. We won't mention the whole poppy field incident.

Fine. I fell asleep. It could have happened to anyone. I AM rather small, you know, and it doesn't take much for unnatural substances to get into my system. At least they didn't have to go back for me with a few thousand mice, unlike SOME Lions that I could name.

In the end, we got to the Emerald City. I'm not really sure why they made me wear the green spectacles. I suppose that it totally escaped them that dogs are color-blind. To me it wasn't Emerald at all, it was just different shades of grey, which is just like life in general when you stop to think about it.

I had my suspicions about that so-called Wizard the first time that we met him, but I kept them to myself. I knew that he was just getting us out of the way with the whole quest to kill the Wicked

Witch of the West, but I couldn't do anything about it at the time. I made up my mind to get it over with as quickly as possible and once we got to the Witch's castle, I kept my eyes open. Now, I would like to say that I knew she would melt if she were splashed with water, but I really didn't know it ahead of time. I just knew that she really needed a bath. The woman reeked, and it wasn't just because I have a super-sensitive nose. She never washed, which is what you would expect of someone who melts at the touch of water, and it was really obvious if you got downwind of her at all.

I had gotten sick of living in the stink, and so made plans. The Witch would come and check on Dorothy, to see if she was doing her chores quickly enough. I found a bucket that someone had filled with water and managed to get it by the handle. There was a walkway around the kitchen where the Witch could watch if she chose, in order to issue punishments to the Winkies who weren't working to her satisfaction. Knowing that she would be in to check on Dorothy, I set the bucket right at the edge of the walkway above where the girl was working and when the Witch came in, I tipped it over.

Yes, I know that the story you heard was that Dorothy threw a bucket of water on the Witch, but what did you expect her to say? That she was on the floor, crying because the Witch had stolen one of her silver shoes, and while she was busy snivelling, her dog saved her life? Again? Who would want to tell THAT story about themselves?

Anyway, after recovering from the whole ordeal, we went back to the Emerald City and met with the Wizard again. That is the one part of the story that Dorothy got partially right. I knocked over the screen that the Wizard was hiding behind, but not because the Lion's roar scared me, rather because I'd seen the Wizard's feet and could smell him hiding back there and wanted them all to know what was really going on. I tried to tell them, but no one understood me. They could understand lions and mice, but not a single word I said.

After that it was decided that we would be escorted home by the Wizard, who happened to be a balloonist from our own region. Dorothy sewed the balloon while I supervised, making her tear out a few sections where her stitches weren't fine enough. I wasn't sure this was going to work, but it made her happy to think that she was doing something to get us home, so I went along with it. In the meantime, I took speaking lessons from the guard dogs in the City's kennels. I was just staring to get the hang of it too!

About a week later they announced that they were ready to try this crazy contraption. There was a huge fire and the Wizard arranged the balloon so that the hot air billowed into it. I watched with growing trepidation as it filled.

All right, so I have a small fear of heights. There. I admit it. Are you happy now? What rational being wants to ride in a laundry basket that is suspended in the air by more hot air? It doesn't make sense, and we'd already had one insane ride through the skies. I had absolutely no desire to try this again. There was still another Good Witch that we hadn't talked to, and there were ALWAYS other options for getting across the desert. Dorothy didn't even bother to explore them. She just jumped onto the first idea to present itself. You would think that she would have learned from the whole Wicked Witch of the West episode, but no, there we were again, listening to this stupid so-called Wizard. So I ran away until the balloon had taken off. I can't help it that I'm the only smart one in the bunch, really.

Sure, I felt bad for Dorothy. I knew how much she wanted to go home, but there had to be another way. And sure enough, there was! It took one more small trip to see the last Witch who was more than quick enough to help us. Personally, I think that with the Wizard and all of the other Witches out of the way, she had her eye on filling the power vacuum but was afraid that we would be in her way. But with her help we finally came home to Kansas and things returned to normal. In some ways, I'm glad to be in the proper world again, where everyone acts as they ought to act. There is part of me, though, that really wishes we had stayed in Oz because I'm sure that I would have learned to talk by now, and you would all actually understand this story. As it is, I've no doubt wasted my breath and will get yelled at for barking too much again.

We definitely should have stayed in Oz.

About the Author

Melyssa was born and raised on the southern edge of Lake Ontario in the Western New York town of Sodus. Melyssa began voraciously reading (her mother's exact words) at the age of four as an escape from watching apple trees grow, and hasn't stopped yet.

A trip to the town library always followed the Saturday Morning Bowling League, and Melyssa went home each week with as many books as the librarian and her parents allowed. The day she wandered out of the children's section and into the regular fiction has been permanently etched in her mind by the searing strands of Thread falling from the sky and the Dragons who flew to fight them. With the realization that imagination is limitless, she has since been fascinated with Fantasy and Science Fiction.

Melyssa is the Executive Assistant to the owner of a small residential construction company. Her organizational skills are tested daily by her ADHD Boss, her ADHD Husband, her ADHD Cats, and the random things they each leave lying around where they finish using them. When not working or writing, Melyssa sings with The Womens' Chorus of Dallas, manages a haunted attraction at a Halloween Theme Park, makes magic real as a Kitchen Witch, collects an endless supply of cooking magazines, and takes more photos than she can possibly hope to process in her lifetime.

Suffer Not a Witch to Live in Kansas

Steven-Elliot Altman

Lorelei lived on the border of the great desert and the land of the Munchkins, with her guardian, Aunt East, the Wicked Witch of the East. Their castle was damp from the blood, sweat, and tears of the Munchkins who built it, many of whom had died in the process. Aunt East had ruled over the Munchkins since long before Lorelei was born. "Someone ought to burn that Witch," Lorelei would hear when she walked among them, invisible. But if that was the best the malformed midgets had, Aunt East would be safe forever, because Witches could not burn. Let the ungrateful wretches grumble.

Lorelei had known she was special since the tender age of six, when the Witch of the East took her from the orphanage to become her apprentice. At fourteen, Lorelei was well on her way to becoming a Witch herself. What marvelous fun they had, Lorelei and Aunt East, hunting together after midnight for the perfect mandrake root, or gathering up the most potent poppies at dawn. There were vision quests and voodoo quests, bonfires and broom rides. Their laughter echoed across the skies of Oz.

Now Aunt East was green from weariness, working from dusk until dawn casting spells with Aunt West, the Wicked Witch of the West, to destroy the foul Wizard in his Emerald City.

But Prospero always made Lorelei smile. Prospero was not green. He was brown, with slender black wings, clever eyes, and tiny teeth set in a devilish grin. The runt of the flock of Winged Monkeys enslaved by Aunt West, Prospero had been given to Lorelei as a familiar, on the condition that each week he fly back to Aunt West to report on Lorelei's progress. The arrangement suited Lorelei and Prospero perfectly. The two of them made fine companions; they played all day long and loved each other dearly.

Then one morning Lorelei awoke and looked out her turret and saw a rainbow, a terrible omen. And Prospero shouted, "The Witch of the West is coming!"

Fluttering several feet above her head, he descended to Lorelei's right shoulder, tangling one wing in her pigtails and digging his toes into her skin.

"You're pinching me, Prospero!" Lorelei exclaimed. "Remind me to cut your nails."

From the turret she saw Aunt West approaching swiftly on her broomstick. A crash of thunder rocked the skies.

The girl rushed down the long, spiral stone staircase, with Prospero flapping nervously behind her, then ran outside to find Aunt East, already waiting. Aunt West caught her footing and handed her broomstick to Lorelei, towering over her niece.

"Come, sister," she commanded Aunt East, "we have things to speak of. Victory is within our grasp!"

She turned to Lorelei, bending to stroke her cold fingers against Lorelei's warm, alabaster cheek.

"You, too, my pretty," she cackled. "The time has come to earn your keep."

Aunt West went to her sister's scrying glass and passed a hand over the murky globe. As images began to form, she told Lorelei what she needed to know.

"Once upon a time, there arose two shadow worlds, with very different natural laws. One clasped to the bosom of magic, while the other suckled a thing called science. Look, Lorelei, and behold . . ."

The image in the glass solidified into a girl running along a dirt road beneath a vast gray sky. A small, filthy dog barked and nipped at her heels. Lorelei gasped. The girl looked exactly like her, right down to the pigtails and freckles.

"Dorothy is your doppelganger in Kansas," Aunt West explained. "Each of us has one. I have one, your Aunt East has one, and the Wizard has one, too. In fact, the Wizard we know *is* the doppelganger. He came to Oz airborne, in a scientific device called a Balloon, and when he did, the law of balance forced his twin back to his place of origin."

The image in the glass shifted. Lorelei saw a white-haired man in a frilly suit, with a bald head and wrinkled face, building a campfire. He looked just like the Wizard.

"Long ago we realized that the Wizard was a powerless man in this world, possessing no natural magic," Aunt West continued. "Having mastered no wizardry to compensate, he used smoke and mirrors to charm and frighten the dimwitted citizens of Emerald City. What made him our master was the thunderstick he brought with him. If there were no gunpowder in Oz, there would be no Wizard, either. The introduction of that curse into our world was the greatest sin ever perpetrated on us. Gunpowder has been responsible for the slaughter of thousands, perhaps tens of thousands of Oz citizens, and it is up to the three of us to punish him for his crime. And who has more right to do so than you? Put these on, child."

Aunt West handed Lorelei a small bundle of faded clothes.

Lorelei removed her black silk cloak and underthings, grappling to believe that Kansas actually existed, was not merely a tale Munchkins told their young to frighten them into behaving but a real, desolate land *without magic*. And Aunt West was determined to send her to this hell. As she struggled into the white-and-blue-checked gingham dress identical to what Dorothy was wearing, she asked Aunt West, "Are you telling me that the man who killed my parents is from Kansas?"

"Several days' journey from there," Aunt West said. "A place called Omaha. But Kansas is where he is now, quite near to where your doppelganger Dorothy lives. He's a false prophet traveling with a carnival that changes location on a near daily basis, and he's preparing to leave soon for an even more distant country. So the time to act is now. We may never have you this close again."

Aunt East helped Lorelei fasten up the dress, and tied the pink sunbonnet on her head. Lorelei frowned, glaring at her reflection in the mirror.

"This outfit is hideous."

"You need to blend in with your surroundings," Aunt West said. "They must believe you are Dorothy. Once you arrive, arm yourself as quickly as possible. The Wizard will never expect an ambush in Kansas. When he dies, so shall his doppelganger."

"But I've never killed anything," Lorelei protested. "How can I hope to kill the Wizard?"

"That is your task, my pretty," Aunt West said. "You must overcome the unfortunate tenderness you sometimes display."

"I believe in you, Lorelei," said Aunt East. "If you use the skills we've taught you, I know you can do it."

"Can Prospero come with me?"

"He'd draw far too much attention," Aunt West said. "There are no Winged Monkeys in Kansas. Our success requires surprise."

"But even if I succeed, how will I get back to Oz?"

"There's no time to explain. Just follow my directions and kill the Wizard," was the Witch of the West's implacable response.

Lorelei turned to Aunt East for support, but Aunt East too was powerless against Aunt West. She took Lorelei's hand tenderly in her own.

"You leave that to us, dear. We'll grab Dorothy the moment she arrives in Oz. She'll be harmless here, and we'll see to it that no harm befalls her. Once the Wizard is no more, we'll use the power of the silver shoes I'm wearing to summon you home."

Lorelei looked into Aunt East's eyes and nodded, resigned. The plan was simple, but carrying it out would take brains, heart, and courage. The future of Oz rested on her shoulders. Lorelei doubted she'd survive, much less succeed.

But first they had to make the switch.

Lorelei mounted the broomstick behind Aunt East and wrapped her arms tightly around her waist. The Witches rose in the air above the courtyard and began to circle the castle, Aunt West on the outside, flying clockwise, Aunt East and Dorothy on the inside, flying counter-clockwise, increasing speed as they circled, with Aunt West and Aunt East chanting the Charm of Making. Hot winds stung Lorelei's eyes; her pigtails came undone and lashed about her. Faster and faster they flew. Aunt West became a blur. Lorelei clung desperately to Aunt East.

They'd conjured a cyclone.

Aunt West departed, soaring upward out of the funnel as Aunt East flew them into the calm center and began their descent, pitching their broom downward and downward, toward a small farmhouse far below.

Lorelei imagined she saw the house begin to shake. Suddenly it dislodged from the ground and was spinning, whirling upward, growing larger and larger as it raced directly at them.

Lorelei screamed and blacked out.

When she opened her eyes again, she was plummeting downward. Tiny wings strained to bear her weight against the violent buffeting. She realized she was being carried. Prospero, who rarely did as he was told, had followed them and, at the last possible moment, snatched Lorelei off the back of Aunt East's broomstick before the house could dash them to their deaths.

Eventually, they tumbled down amid a cloud of hot, swirling dust, suffering little more than a bump to Lorelei's head. They looked at the carnage: the crushed barn, dead animals, and debris strewn as far as the eye could see. The cyclone and farmhouse were gone.

Where was Aunt East?

A gut-wrenching pain gripped Lorelei, doubling her over, onto her knees. She heaved into the cracked Kansas dust.

"What's happening to me, Prospero?" she cried.

The monkey tried his best to comfort Lorelei, pulling her hair from her face and patting her gently on the back. Suddenly the Witch of the East's bloodstone ring appeared on the middle finger of Lorelei's right hand, and Prospero understood.

"It's a transfer of power," he whispered softly into Lorelei's ear. "Unfortunately, it means your Aunt is dead. You are now the Witch of the East."

Lorelei burst into tears. And then she heard Aunt West's voice.

"This is no time for tears, girl. Your Aunt East wanted only two things in life: to see you grow to one day fill her shoes, and to see you slay the Wizard. Now the day has come and you have the power to fulfill her fondest wish. Armed with that ring you may utter the Charm of Making. You must not let her down."

"Dorothy! Dorothy, where are you?" a woman's voice called in the distance.

"The girl's Aunt Em and Uncle Henry are searching for her. They can't see you until I let them. You mustn't fail us. Get up. Be their Dorothy. Arm yourself and find the Wizard—and hide that disobedient monkey!"

"Dorothy, where are you, girl?" came a man's plaintive voice, close by now.

Lorelei could no longer sense her Aunt West's presence.

"There she is!" Uncle Henry yelled.

She turned to Prospero and quickly sketched a figure in the air with two extended fingers of her right hand, which rendered the monkey invisible just before a group of farmhands rushed to hug and kiss her. Lorelei found their affection disquieting.

"I feared you were lost," Uncle Henry said, squeezing her as though he might never let go. "Where's Toto?"

"Toto?" Lorelei asked, and froze, fearing she'd given herself away.

"Your dog, Dorothy," Aunt Em said. "Where is the poor dog?"

"I have no idea, Aunt Em. I hit my head."

She offered her head for inspection.

"Oh dear, Henry. She has hit her head, and her scalp is cold. We'd better take her to the cellar to lie down."

They brought Lorelei to where the house had stood and led her into the cellar, where they settled her on a hay-filled mattress. The other farmhands went to find out which, if any, stock had survived. Aunt Em took Lorelei's right hand.

"Dorothy, where did you get that strange ring?" she asked.

"I found it," Lorelei said, bringing the hand to her heart and covering it with her other hand.

"Well, it looks to be cutting off your circulation. Let's take it off for now."

She tried to coax the ring from Lorelei's finger. It would not come off, no matter how much Aunt Em pushed, twisted, or tugged it. She did not know that only Lorelei's death would make removing it possible. But Lorelei knew, and whimpered at the reminder of how the ring had come to her.

"There, there," Aunt Em said. "I'll leave the ring be."

"I want to go home," Lorelei said weakly.

"I'm afraid our home is gone, Dorothy. Nearly everything we had was lost in the cyclone. We're all lucky to have survived, to still have each other. That's what truly matters. We'll build a new house soon enough. Won't we, Henry?"

This was a nightmare. Lorelei needed to wake up. She needed to . . . arm herself and find the Wizard, the man who killed her parents, and then kill him, in order to leave this miserable place and go back to Oz, her *real* home.

Something touched her face lightly, startling Lorelei. Imperceptibly, she reached and felt Prospero's invisible hand, and squeezed it in relief.

A new, burly farmhand rushed into the cellar to report how coming back from town he'd seen the traveling carnival had been destroyed.

"They got hit bad. Wagons flipped on their sides and dead animals everywhere. Saw a dead elephant."

The farmhand had tears in his eyes. Aunt West would have called him weak, crying over an animal that couldn't even talk.

"That ain't all," the farmhand said. "Handler I spoke to said there's more animals loose. They're mostly tame, but the longer they go without food, the wilder they'll get."

"We'd best go and see if we can help," Uncle Henry said.

"But Henry," Aunt Em said, "we got plenty troubles of our own right here."

"You know it's the Lord's will that we help those in need greater than our own, Em. We're all alive and we got enough food stored to last weeks. Don't you worry. We'll take lanterns and rifles and we'll help round up what's left. Likely we'll be back before dark."

Doing something in the name of kindness toward strangers seemed quite mad to Lorelei. It brought to mind the time an old woman had come to Aunt East to beg a favor. A woodman was trying to steal her only daughter, and she wanted him stopped. Aunt East had decided the request was just, and she'd enchanted the woodman's axe so that it slipped, cutting him limb from limb. In return, she'd made the woman give up her best sheep. And after all, the woodman had replaced his limbs with tin ones. Didn't these people understand the principle of balance? But the mention of the carnival and rifles had got her attention.

"See that you're back safe, is all," Aunt Em said, and sent the men on their way.

Lorelei attempted to get up, but Aunt Em stopped her.

"Where do you think you're going, young lady?"

"To the carnival . . . to help Uncle Henry."

"That's men's work, Dorothy. You stay right here and rest."

Lorelei sighed and lay back, turning her head to whisper in Prospero's invisible ear.

"Follow them and see where they keep their weapons."

Not long after the men had left, Aunt Em fell asleep. Lorelei was out of the cellar in moments.

Night was fast approaching. "Prospero, reveal yourself," Lorelei commanded. She snapped her fingers, and the Winged Monkey appeared, hovering a few feet from where she stood. "Show me what you've found."

Flapping briskly, Prospero led Lorelei to a small wooden shed that had somehow managed to remain standing. Leaning against a wall was a wooden scythe with a sharp steel blade. Lorelei took it outside and swung the blade several times to get the weight and slice just right. It was perfect.

They set off to kill the Wizard along the dusty, debris-strewn road away from the farm. Before long Lorelei noticed a broken tree with a ragged poster still pinned to it, indicating the direction of the carnival. Lorelei pined for the dazzling colors of Oz as they passed row after row of unending, colorless cornfields.

"Look over there," Prospero said, indicating a tall pole in the center of the closest cornfield. "A moment ago, I saw a scarecrow hanging off it. Now it's gone."

If Prospero, with his keen animal senses and instincts, was scared – as indeed it seemed – she took it seriously, for Prospero was no cowardly monkey and they knew not the laws of this forsaken place.

"Let's keep moving and try to stay ahead of it," she whispered.

Lorelei swung the scythe before her as they walked. Every now and again a few stalks of corn would rustle for no apparent reason, just ahead of or behind them, always out of their direct sight, despite the fact that there was no wind.

Suddenly a scarecrow twice her size leapt at Lorelei from the cornfield. Prospero pulled Lorelei away, frantically flapping his wings as she struggled to raise the scythe in their defense. The Scarecrow tumbled jaggedly forward, then rose and spun to face them. Its head was a small sack stuffed with straw, with eyes, nose, and mouth painted on it in a terrible stare. An old, pointed hat perched on his head. The rest of the figure was a suit of clothes, worn and faded, which had also been stuffed with straw. It made no sound as it advanced on Lorelei. She swung the scythe in warning. The gruesome thing fearlessly staggered forward, jabbing its fingers at her. Still, she could not believe it was capable of doing her any real harm.

Until it got a grip on one of her pigtails, and yanked her head with considerable force, thrusting its straw fingers against her face like sharp pins – and Lorelei felt warm blood break her skin.

She swung the scythe wide and sliced the wretched Scarecrow at the waist. It fell to the ground in two piles – and then its arms shot out and Lorelei watched, incredulous, as it dragged its upper half to join its lower half, stuffed itself together, and began to rise again.

Lorelei sheared the Scarecrow's head off, so hard that it rolled several yards away. The body went down on its knees and scrambled around searching for the head.

What was animating the creature? Supposedly there was no magic in Kansas. If it wasn't the spirit of the place, it must be the Wizard. That meant he knew she was coming for him. Even worse, he was capable of true wizardry, and Aunt West had been wrong. If this terrifying Scarecrow was his then it was here either to kill her or at the very least to test her and send her away in defeat. None of these options was acceptable.

The sack of putrid mold and hay reassembled itself and turned once more in their direction. As it shambled into range, Lorelei determined that *Fire scorches Wood* and cast the Charm of Making for her very first time, saying "Pyrocombustium!"

Aunt East's bloodstone glowed green on Lorelei's hand. The brass setting bit hard against her finger as a ball of fire appeared. She plunged it into the Scarecrow's chest just as its gnarled hands grasped for her throat.

The Scarecrow's stuffing caught fire and the smoldering mass danced a ludicrous jig as it tried to dash out the flames. Lorelei and Prospero each tore off a limb and fed them to the fire. The first and only sound it ever made was the *crackle* and *hiss* of its own burning body.

Lorelei stamped out the fire. She handed the Scarecrow's head – all that was left – to Prospero and bade him fly back to the pole and place it there as both a punishment and warning.

"See how you enjoy living without a body, foul creature," she sneered. "And tell the Wizard that Lorelei, the Witch of the East, shall not be stopped."

The moon had risen. The road grew slower and more difficult, for it was littered with split and toppled trees, and though Prospero could easily flutter over any obstacle, he was too weary to carry Lorelei, who had to climb over or crawl under each one. She wondered if the cyclone had caused this, or if the Wizard had put them there to deter her.

She noticed a curious dwelling half buried by a fallen tree. Maybe they could rest there. Prospero flew ahead to check for danger, and signaled it was safe.

The front door had been blown off; no one was home. Inside they found vegetables in wooden crates, jars filled with fruits, and grains and seeds in metal bins.

"It must be a trading post," Lorelei decided. "Let's see what they have to offer."

Prospero found a blanket and laid it on the floor, Lorelei found some candles, and they set out a proper picnic. The food was welcome and fresh enough for consumption, but everything was bland, or utterly tasteless.

The next thing they found was a large glass-top cabinet filled with thundersticks. Lorelei pulled one out. The metal was heavy and cold. A machine like this had killed her parents. Part of her wanted to drop it right there and have nothing more to do with it, but part of her wanted to learn how to use it, so she could use it on the Wizard. The balance was fitting.

She searched until she found a box of the little metal gunpowder containers the thundersticks discharged, with a picture that looked just like the weapon she'd chosen. She followed the directions, pressing the lever that broke open the breech and loading the gun with two shells, one in each barrel, bending the stock and barrel back into a straight line to close the breech, and snapped the gun closed. According to the box, it was now ready to fire. She raised it in both hands, and continued reading as she cradled the weapon.

Aim the shotgun and follow your target until you are ready to take your shot. With your fingers positioned over the two triggers, pull your lead finger first to fire. This will fire one shell. If you want to fire the second, pull the other trigger.

Lorelei had one eye closed and was sighting down the barrel when she noticed the shadow of a man in the far corner of the room.

"Who are you and why are you hiding?" she demanded. "I warn you, I have a gun and I've just learned how to use it."

The man did not reply.

Prospero and Lorelei crept closer, gun raised and scythe at the ready, until they were close enough to see that it wasn't a real man but a metal statue. His tin hands clutched a small glass bowl filled with sweets. He was nearly rusted through, and *Rust corrupts Metal*, she knew.

Lorelei decided to be cautious. She pointed the thunderstick at the statue's chest, right where its heart should be, lest he suddenly spring to life. There was something familiar about him. The ring pulsed as she laid her right hand against the cold, coarse, rusted tin of his face, to see if her new powers could reveal what it was.

"This statue is a doppelganger, Prospero! A Kansas version of the woodman Aunt East cursed for attempting to steal the old woman's daughter."

A small, sharp flake of rust upon its face pierced the pulpy flesh of Lorelei's right index finger. Lorelei winced, and pulled her hand away. No blood had been shed; there was nothing to worry about.

Suddenly tired, Lorelei made herself a bed of blankets beneath the Tin Woodman, and with Prospero curled beside her soon fell into a sound sleep.

Ever so slightly, the Woodman smiled.

The next morning they ate a small, tasteless breakfast before heading off again. Lorelei carried the thunderstick, as well as a pocketful of shells. Prospero fluttered along, the scythe across his shoulders. The weather was clear and pleasant as the road diverged through the woods. Another carnival flyer informed them that they were going the right way.

Lorelei kept examining her right index finger, where she'd been pricked.

"Does it hurt?" Prospero asked.

"More than one would expect. I've salved it twice already with woundwort I found, but it keeps throbbing. I hope it gets better soon."

Within an hour it had grown worse and Lorelei's entire hand was numb.

"Is there something I can do, Lorelei?" Prospero asked. "You look feverish."

"I feel like I desperately need water," she said. "I'm practically trembling, and it's quite painful when I swallow."

"But water—"

"I know, Prospero. *Water dissolves Magic.* Now that I'm a Witch, the Charm of Making will be my undoing if I drink water. Maybe some tree sap can help."

Prospero found a broken tree that readily gave up its sap. Lorelei wadded the viscous substance into a blob and chewed it, which seemed to soothe the pain a little. She felt oddly compelled to thank the tree.

Then the muscles tightened in Lorelei's right forearm. Pain constricted the hand; her fingers curled into a claw that neither she nor Prospero could straighten. What was happening to her in this nightmarish place? Lorelei hated Kansas.

Eventually the spasms subsided, leaving Lorelei winded and shaky. Prospero could do nothing to aid her, which troubled him gravely. "I'll figure out some way to heal this," Lorelei reassured him. She wished she believed it herself.

A deep growl sounded. Lorelei's heart beat fast.

Prospero sniffed the air. "Lion," he said. "A big one." He fluttered close at Lorelei's side, scythe held ready. Lorelei kept the thunderstick close.

They'd wandered off the road. The ground was covered with dried branches and dead leaves. They quickened their pace, each cursed crunch of leaves beneath her feet a signal to the enemy. Just as they dared to think they might be safe, there came another growl, much closer.

"It's got our scent," Prospero whispered. "Maybe you should fire a shot to scare him."

But it was too late; the great Lion was upon them. With one swipe of his paw he sent the screeching Winged Monkey spinning head over heels to smash against a tree. Then he lunged at Lorelei, who emptied both barrels of the thunderstick into him, hammering him backward as a tremendous spray of blood splattered Lorelei.

The big cat roared ferociously, then retreated into the woods.

Lorelei rushed to her familiar.

"Please tell me you're all right, Prospero! You must be. You can't leave me to face the Wizard alone."

Prospero opened his eyes and smiled.

"That was very brave, Lorelei. I believe you are the most courageous girl I have ever known. I'm honored to be your friend."

Lorelei hugged him tightly, despite her own pain. "Are you all right enough to fly?" she asked. "I want you to see if you can locate the carnival."

Prospero did as Lorelei requested. "We are very close," he reported. "Not ten minutes away."

Lorelei was unsure if she could walk even that far. Her right arm had gone numb, her jaw ached, and her legs were stiff.

"I'll fly you there, Lorelei," Prospero said.

The Winged Monkey carefully placed his arms beneath Lorelei's armpits, around her chest. Lorelei held the thunderstick and scythe as tightly as possible. Straining his wings, Prospero lifted them skyward. Soon they could make out a clearing littered with the wreckage of the carnival the burly farmhand had described in the cellar. That seemed so long ago to Lorelei. There were fallen tents, overturned coaches, and dead animals strewn in every direction. All was still, save for the gentle music of an unseen calliope. They began their descent.

With a grunt, Prospero set them on the ground, roughly yet safely. Lorelei handed Prospero the scythe and stiffly reloaded the thunderstick, hoping she had enough power to face the Wizard. She was limping now. Her strength was fading fast. They moved toward the sound of the calliope.

As they rounded a collapsed tent, they encountered a man who sat on the ground looking dazed and confused. His face was painted deathly white. He had a small rubber nose affixed to his own, and wore the most garish clothing Lorelei had ever seen, including shoes that were five sizes too big for him. He must be of Munchkin descent. But how was that possible? The queer fellow gasped at the sight of Prospero.

Lorelei aimed the thunderstick and demanded, "Take us to the Wizard!"

"You mean the Oracle? You don't want to bother him, ma'am. He's lost everything on account of that twister."

Lorelei cocked both triggers.

"Surely, ma'am, right this way. Quite a monkey ya got there."

The Munchkin led them to one of the few tents still standing, and scurried away. Inside they found the little old man in a frilly suit with bald head and wrinkled face that Lorelei had seen in Aunt East's scrying glass.

"Why Lorelei, I'm surprised to see you here," he said.

Lorelei aimed the thunderstick at the Wizard. "That's a lie," she said, her jaw so tight it hurt to speak. "Tell me it wasn't you who animated the Scarecrow and poisoned the Tin Woodman, or sent the Lion to kill us."

"That was me," he confessed. "But I did so in self-defense, as you well know. And it seems I've failed. What I meant was that I was surprised to see you survived the Lion. I must say, you've proven much more clever and courageous than I imagined. Just like your doppelganger, Dorothy."

"How do you know all this?" Lorelei demanded. Her breath was so labored it hurt to breathe. "How do you know my name? Or about Dorothy? Or even that I was sent here to kill you?"

"I know because I am the Oracle of Omaha, just as I am the Wizard of Oz. Once I made peace with that fact, I learned to share information with my other self, who after all is me. Two heads are much better than one, my dear. There are bridges between worlds that are easily crossed, if one wishes to cross them. The Wizard knows Dorothy because, like you, she embarked on a journey and found her way to him.

"I'll tell you what else I know, Lorelei. I know that you're dying.

You've little time left. And if you die, so shall Dorothy. Most important of all, I know how to cure you."

Lorelei's eyes widened.

"That's right," the Wizard said. "How does it feel to wield the Charm of Making, to know you can conjure the cure for any illness, save your own?"

"Cut off his head," Lorelei croaked to Prospero.

"Wait one second!" the old man cried. "You haven't allowed me to offer you my bargain. I'm sure you'll want to consider it, as it involves not only saving your life but claiming vengeance for the deaths of your parents."

Lorelei placed the barrel of the gun against the Wizard's chest.

"You killed my parents, old man," she hissed.

"The Witches would have you believe that, of course," he replied. "But what if I told you your father was killed by a pack of Gray Wolves, and your mother by a swarm of Black Bees. Would that mean anything to you?"

It would mean Aunt West had killed her parents.

Lorelei tried to shout, "You're lying," but her jaw would barely move. Her skull felt like it was being consumed by cold fire.

"Put nothing past the Wicked Witch of the West, Lorelei. She killed your parents to make you an orphan, then sent your Aunt East to raise you as she dictated, all the while poisoning you against me and grooming you for this very day. But she never counted on my discovering her plan and revealing it to you. You have Dorothy to thank for that. It was her courage that led me to comprehend the plot against me. You only believe you are removed from Dorothy's goodness because you've been lied to all your life. Remember all the things you've been told over the years that didn't quite ring true, all the loving instincts you tried to bury, but never quite could?"

Lorelei's world was spinning out of control. But there was something to what the old man told her. Painfully she cocked both triggers of the thunderstick and raised it to the Wizard's head.

"Prove it, Wizard, or you die right now."

"He can't prove any of it, Lorelei!"

Aunt West's malevolent voice rang out, as the image of her disembodied head appeared high in the tent above them.

"Kill him and I shall bring you back to Oz and cure you. In the name of our beloved Aunt East, kill him now!"

"Think, Lorelei," the old man countered. "Think with your heart.

Show her you have the courage to figure this out for yourself. She says she can cure you. Ask her what sickness ails you."

Lorelei looked up at Aunt West's head. It was clear she did not know the answer.

"It's called tetanus, Lorelei," the Wizard said. "For you it's curable only one way. Use the charm they taught you to suffer a Witch. Ask her how she intends to bring you home to Oz, now that Dorothy owns the silver shoes."

Aunt West's mouth fell open in outrage, but all Lorelei's attention was on the Wizard.

"Open your mind to Dorothy, Lorelei. Ask her if your Aunt West has not been attempting to murder her in Oz. You know what happens to you if your doppelganger dies."

"Don't you dare try to communicate with Dorothy!" Aunt West screamed. *"I forbid it!"*

"It's a simple spell, Lorelei," the Wizard continued. "Just repeat to yourself, *I am you and you are me, and I can see what you can see. You are me and I am you, and I must know all that you do.*"

Lorelei's entire being was pain as she muttered the spell. Suddenly it was as if she were two people at once: Lorelei, standing before the Wizard in Kansas with a gun to his head, and Dorothy, mop in hand, facing the Wicked Witch of the West in her castle in Oz, who just this moment was attempting to steal her silver shoes. And because Dorothy knew Aunt West was lying, Lorelei also knew it.

"It matters little if you know the truth now, wretched girl!" Aunt West snarled. *"You'll both be dead in moments. Yes, I killed your parents. Now Prospero, my fine slave, by the power of Quelala's Golden Cap, I command you to kill the Wizard!"*

The infection in Lorelei's body finally overcame her, systematically shutting down her nervous system. Her legs went first. She fell to her knees and dropped the gun. She looked at her familiar, hovering with the scythe poised to strike the Wizard. Prospero glanced back in torment.

"Whatever you choose to do, Prospero, I shall always love you!" she whispered, fearing they were her final words.

Suddenly Prospero was snatched from the air in the slamming jaws of the Lion, who had been all but forgotten. Wounded but having life within him still, the dumb beast could do nothing short of completing its mission. Prospero died screeching.

Lorelei closed her eyes and was no longer Lorelei, crippled and unable to move, but Dorothy, confronting Aunt West in the castle's kitchen. The Witch of the West held her broomstick up, poised for a deathstrike. With no time to explain her plan to Dorothy or seek her acceptance, Lorelei cast a charm and took control of Dorothy's body.

Aunt West recognized the change immediately.

"Well, my pretty. It seems your time has come."

"Yes, Aunt West," Dorothy replied with Lorelei's voice as she threw down the mop. "And now at last your wicked days are done."

Lorelei picked up the bucket of water that stood near Dorothy's side and soaked Aunt West from head to foot. With a loud cry of fear, the Witch began to shrink and fall away.

In Kansas, Lorelei once more experienced the gut-wrenching pain that doubled her over, and began heaving. Aunt West's moonstone ring appeared on the middle finger of her left hand. The Wicked Witch of the West was dead.

Purged of sickness by the surge of power, Lorelei discovered that she could readily stand. She rose up and gazed sadly at Prospero's body.

"Thank you, Lorelei," the Wizard said, bowing low. "With both my mortal enemies vanquished, I may rule Oz unopposed. But first I must know, since you are now both the Witch of the East and the West, are you a good Witch, or a bad Witch?"

"I'm not sure," Lorelei answered, pointing the gun at the Wizard. "But now Dorothy and I are both wondering if this wasn't your plan all along."

The Wizard chuckled nervously.

"You had better return to Oz with me," she decided.

"Now Dorothy, listen closely. I need you to knock your heels together three times, and repeat after me."

About the Author

Steven-Elliot Altman is a bestselling author, Hollywood screenwriter, and most recently a successful videogame developer, having won multiple awards for his online role playing game *9Dragons*. Steven's novels include *Captain America is Dead, Zen in the Art of Slaying Vampires, Batman: Fear Itself, Batman: Infinite Mirror, The Killswitch Review, The Irregulars* and *Deprivers*. In reviews of note his writing has been compared to that of Stephen King, Dean Koontz, Michael Crichton and Philip K. Dick, and he has collaborated with world class writers such as Neil Gaiman, Michael Reaves, Harry Turtledove and Dr. Janet Asimov. He's also the editor of the critically acclaimed anthology *The Touch* and a contributor to *Shadows Over Baker Street*, a Hugo Award winning anthology of Sherlock Holmes meets H.P. Lovecraft stories. Steve is currently hard at work writing and directing his latest videogame *Cursed Love*, an online free to play gothic horror RPG from Dark Hermit Studios, set in Victorian London. Find *Cursed Love* on facebook and you can have fun playing with Steve while the game is being beta tested!

The Munchkin Boy

Tim Frayser

The Munchkin boy to the fields had gone
To gather grain for his fam'ly
The summer days had been hot and long
And the fields were yielding their crops badly

But as he walked did a tempest strike
With wind and rain and thunder
The Munchkin boy hid with much dislike
Lest his body be blown all asunder

When the Munchkin boy did at last arise
A different land spread out before him
The stalks of grain they were twice his size
In long rows tall and bright and golden

Quickly then did his knife's edge turn
And soon, a healthy sheaf was bundled
But then, he wondered how he would return
To the distant land from which he tumbled

On a distant hill did he spy the storm
And soon he rushed back to it's terrors
The winds were scary but when blue skies formed
He was back in happy Munchkin acres

Back home, his fam'ly they did plant his seeds
And prospered bountiful and boisterous
From then therafter would his title be
"The shortest farmer in all Kansas."

About the Poet

Tim Frayser has been telling stories his whole life. A writer, cartoonist, martial artist, ordained minister and traveler, he also volunteers as a Black Rock Ranger at the annual Burning Man festival in Nevada. He lives in Broken Arrow, Oklahoma.

East of the Sun, West of the Moon

Tracy S. Morris

When Dorothy heard splintering wood in the next bedroom, she knew that Susan found a pry bar from somewhere. The sounds gave way to scuffling noises. Her door opened and Alice poked her blonde head into the room.

"Susan's tearing up her wardrobe floor. Wendy tried to stop her, and now they're fighting again."

Dorothy put her half-read letter on the table. Aunt Em and news of the farm would just have to wait. She picked up the pail of water that sat by the door as she stepped into the hallway. Outside, Wendy and Susan tugged at either end of the iron bar in a struggle for possession.

"Be sensible, Susan! We're all on probation with Mrs. Lovett. One more violation and we'll all be out on the streets like lost boys!"

"Leave me alone!" Susan yelled at her. "You don't understand! No one does!"

Dorothy rolled her eyes at Susan's histrionics. The entire reason the four of them threw in together was that they were the only ones who did understand one another. She put her thumb and forefinger into her mouth and blew out a shrill blast of air. Instantly, both girls ceased their struggle. "Su?"

"What?" Susan asked in a subdued tone of voice.

Dorothy held up her pail of water so that Susan could see it clearly. "You know what that means don't you?"

With a petulant sound, Susan threw down her end of the bar with a clang and flounced into her room. The sound of distressed bedsprings told Dorothy that she'd probably flopped onto the bed.

"Hide that thing better next time so she can't find it." She ordered. Wendy stuck her tongue out in response.

"Oh very mature," Alice crossed her arms and stuck her nose in the air. "Aren't we all supposed to be adults?"

Dorothy ignored them as she pushed into Susan's room without waiting for an invitation. When she put the bucket down, the other girls sighed in obvious relief.

Dorothy fixed Susan with the look she learned from Aunt Em the day she had to give up her dog Toto. "Why did you attack your wardrobe?"

"Because it's an ordinary wardrobe." Susan's voice sounded muffled from where she buried her head in her pillow. She looked up through her crossed arms with a doe-eyed expression. "Just like everything else in this dull, ordinary, mundane world."

"Her latest beau broke up with her," Wendy whispered behind Dorothy's back.

Susan glared at Wendy over Dorothy's shoulder. "I'm through with dating! Through with lipstick! Through with Nylons and invitations and accepting my lot in this mundane world! It never helps me to forget that I was a queen once."

Alice pushed her way into the room. She sat on the bed and smoothed Susan's hair in a comforting gesture from one Queen to another. Wendy crossed her arms and leaned against the doorway.

Dorothy turned her attention to the wardrobe. The gouges that Susan tore from the furniture were all along one side. Dorothy pushed the worst of the splinters back into place and hung Susan's robe from the corner of the door. She brushed her hands and nodded in satisfaction. At least it would pass one of Mrs. Lovett's cursory inspections. Their landlady was quite a frightening woman, and none of them wanted to consider what she might do if they failed an inspection.

"I wish we did have the luxury of retreating to fantasy land." Dorothy threw her words over her shoulder at the others. Wishing it were so only brought pain. Better to maintain forward momentum in life. "But we're adults now. We have classes to teach. Young minds to mold."

"Ugh," Wendy made a face. "Mundane children have no imagination."

"We could do worse than stretching those young imaginations," Dorothy turned to chide Wendy gently.

Susan sat up in bed, her posture stiff. "Maybe you've given up, but I haven't. I'm going to find a way back." She looked at each of them in turn. "For all of us."

Dorothy decided to change the subject. "I'm afraid that you can't use your robe anymore." She sat on the end of the bed. The springs made a popping sound and the mattress sagged under their combined weight. Before Susan could continue, she changed the subject, "I got a letter from home."

The other three girls looked up in interest. "What's new in Kansas?" Susan asked.

"The railroad is buying out the farm. Uncle Henry wants to take Aunt Em to live with his sister in San Fransisco."

"That's wonderful news!" Alice clapped her hands together. When the other three girls glared at her, she lowered her hands. Her face fell. "Isn't it good news? You don't have to send half your pay back to your aunt."

"I guess." Dorothy picked at a frayed corner of Susan's blanket.

"The whole reason she came back from OZ was to help her Aunt and Uncle take care of their farm. They sent her to get a job and then sold the farm. So . . ." Wendy whispered to Alice in a voice low enough that they thought Dorothy couldn't hear. Dorothy kept her face averted so that they wouldn't think she was eavesdropping.

"Oh!" Alice's voice sounded contrite. "She returned to the mundane world for nothing."

"And she's on her own now, just like us." Susan added in a glum monotone.

Dorothy faced them again to find all three girls looking at her in watery sympathy. She cringed inwardly. "It's fine," she said.

"Look on the bright side," Susan replied. "You can actually afford to eat in the cafeteria instead of subsisting on that horrid soup that you always make."

"And you can go with us to the fair that just opened."

Her stomach rolled at the thought. She had watched the carnival rides rise like leviathans from the deep and seen the testing of the lights. The exposition grounds looked wondrous. As much a marvel as the Emerald City.

"Thank you for inviting me," Dorothy said quietly. "But I'm not sure I can endure the spectacle."

The other three girls traded unhappy looks. "If you change your mind . . ." Alice let the unspoken invitation hang between them.

"Thank you." Dorothy picked up the pail and pry bar and left the room.

"Miss Gayle?"

Dorothy looked up from the sheaf of geography papers to find headmistress Price standing in the doorway.

"Yes Ma'am?" Dorothy raised her own eyebrows. Headmistress

Price rarely took time away from her own correspondence studies to concern herself with the day-to-day running of the school.

"Have you seen Miss Pevensie or Miss Darling today?"

Alice slid from a tiptoed run to stand behind headmistress Price. She waved frantically at Dorothy.

"Aren't they in their classrooms?" She titled her head sideways. "They rode the trolley in with me this morning."

Headmistress Price shook her head. "Their lessons are written on the boards in their rooms, so I assumed that there was some kind of emergency. I have Miss Banks and Miss Longstocking looking in on the classes to make sure that the girls behave. But I thought that since the four of you boarded together, that you might know where they were."

An odd look crossed Headmistress Price's face. As she stepped back to turn on her heel, Alice dove behind the door casing to hide. Headmistress Price looked behind her, shrugged and turned back to the geography classroom.

Dorothy put the papers down, stood and walked to the window, pretending to be fascinated by the empty courtyard below. Where did the two of them go? And how did they manage to go anywhere without an argument? She guessed that she ought to come up with a cover story for them so that they didn't lose their jobs. But the small, spiteful part of her that thought they could be off in Narnia or Neverland without her was tempted to just let them all suffer the consequences.

Her thoughts scattered like a flock of birds when a munchkin dressed all in blue crossed the yard. She caught her breath in surprise.

"Is there something wrong, Miss Gayle?" The headmistress pushed her aside for a better look. "It's just one of the younger girls." Dorothy squinted over Miss Price's shoulder. Now she could see that the small person wasn't a munchkin, but one of the students in a blue school uniform.

"I'm sorry." Dorothy said. "For a moment, she just looked. . . It's not important."

Mrs. Price pressed her hand to Dorothy's forehead. "Are you alright?"

"I have been feeling a bit peaked." Dorothy latched onto the proffered excuse. "Susan wasn't feeling well last night and the four of us sat up with her."

"If she tried to come to school, that would explain where Miss

Darling is. She probably took her back home." Mrs. Price withdrew her hand quickly. Her expression turned suspicious. "If you aren't feeling well, you could spread it to the rest of the school as well." She backed away quickly.

"I can't leave you short handed." Dorothy protested.

"The day is half over anyway." The Headmistress said. "We were going to call a short week so that the girls could go to the fair." She crossed the threshold of Dorothy's entrance and closed the door to the room so that only her head was visible. "Go home, Miss Gayle. Make sure that you and your fellow teachers are all well before you return on Monday." She shut the door behind her with a snick.

Dorothy looked around the room, feeling lost. She picked up her papers and put them into her satchel.

After a moment, Alice slipped into the room. "That was close," She said.

"Did Wendy or Susan say where they were going?" Dorothy put her hands on her hips.

"Not to me." Alice shook her head and held her hands up. "But they did manage to get us excused from class today, so let's not be hard on them."

Dorothy snorted at that. "That depends on what mischief they've gotten into."

Susan was the first one home that night. She practically sang as she wandered the halls to their rooms. As she pulled off her scarf and coat, she noticed Dorothy sulking by the door. "Oh!" She broke off from her singing, eyes widened.

"You're certainly happy," Dorothy crossed her arms. "Whatever you've been up to must have been good. I had to make excuses for you and Wendy with Mrs. Price."

"Wendy?" Susan looked alarmed. "Where is Wendy?"

"I assumed she was with you. Did you manage to find a way into fairyland?."

Susan smiled and looked down. "It wasn't like that, Dorothy. There was a fellow. A wonderful boy."

She considered retrieving her pail of water. "A boy? I thought you were through with lipstick and invitations."

Susan's steps faltered as her expression twisted in horror. "It's not like that. He's just a boy, for heaven's sake! I teach girls older than him. How could I possibly think of him like that?"

"I don't know. You tell me, Susan. You avoided work to spend the day with a boy."

Susan grasped Dorothy's hand with both of her own. "There's nothing improper going on. I took him to a soda fountain and bought him cherry phosphates, just like I would have with my youngest brother. I just wanted to hear his stories. He's like us! And oh what stories!" She spun around with her arms in the air. Then she leaped onto her bed and swished her hand as if fighting with an imaginary sword.

"He's fought pirates! He batted alongside Indians!"

Dorothy grinned in spite of herself. "Where was he from?"

"East of the sun, west of the moon." Susan slid from the bed. "I think maybe he's going to try and go back. He asked me to come with him."

Dorothy's heart sank. "What about the rest of us?"

"I don't know," Susan shrugged. "I haven't asked yet. But surely there is a way for everyone to go."

Dorothy crossed her ankles and leaned against the wall. "Be careful Susan. Stories with adults that journey into fairyland aren't nice like the stories with kids. You don't want to end up like Rip van Winkle. Or Tam Lin."

"I don't care." Susan said quietly. "Anyplace is better than here."

"You can't have him!"

Wendy's yell pierced Dorothy's dreams and sent her bolting out of bed. She swiped at her eyes and collected her bearings. Moonlight streamed into the room, bathing everything in silver.

"Leave me alone!" This time the scream was from Susan. Dorothy frowned. The two girls were once again making enough noise to wake the entire boarding house. As in an echo to her thoughts, Alice stuck her head in the room again. "Dorothy! Bring your bucket!"

Water sloshed over the side of the pail as Dorothy scooped it up. Susan and Wendy stood in the hallway between their two rooms. Susan had a grip on Wendy's nightshirt while Wendy pulled at Susan's hair. Dorothy threw the bucket of water over the both of them, drenching them from head to foot. The two of them recoiled from one another, and Alice slipped between them.

Footsteps behind them alerted Dorothy to the fact that the four of them weren't the only ones awake. She turned to see Mrs. Lovett appear at the head of the stairs, dressed in her robe and carrying a candle.

Mrs. Lovett glared at the four of them and the water pooling under their feet. "What's going on here?"

"Just a difference of opinion," Dorothy said. "We promise to be quieter."

"And we'll clean up the mess, Mrs. Lovett." Alice put in.

Mrs. Lovett looked at each of them with a cold expression. "See that you do. You almost woke Mr. Barker." The old lady turned her nose up, spun on her heel and descended the stairs.

"That was close," Alice hissed at the two of them. "Now what is all of this about?"

"She!" Wendy stabbed the air over Alice's shoulder to indicate Susan. "She's trying to take him away!"

"Him who?" Dorothy snatched her own robe from beside her door and threw it to Susan. Instead of putting it on, Susan used it to mop up the puddle she was standing in.

"Peter Pan!" Wendy threw her words in Susan's face. "I followed you yesterday when you left the school! I don't know what he wants with you, but he was mine first."

Dorothy studied Susan's expression. Her milky complexion turned pale white. "He can't be your Peter. He never once said that he was."

"It makes sense when you think about it." Dorothy rested her chin in her hand. "You said that he's battled pirates."

"But I'm grown!" Susan flopped down on Dorothy's sodden robe. She looked at Wendy with an accusing expression. "You said that he only came to you because you were a child."

"She has a point," Alice put in. "The story always said that Peter Pan refused to grow up. Why would he approach a grown girl?"

"Assuming that it is Peter Pan, why didn't he just talk to one of the school girls? Why approach Susan? For that matter, why not approach Wendy?" Dorothy looked at each of the other girls in turn as she reasoned out loud.

Alice's face lit up with excitement. She raised her hand and waved it like one of her students waiting to be called on. "Oh! Maybe he didn't want Wendy to know he was here?"

"Peter wouldn't do that." Wendy shook her head.

"How do you know?" Dorothy pinned Wendy with a sharp look. "From everything you've told me about Peter, he's a typical little boy — which means that he looks after his own wants and needs before he looks after the feelings of others."

Wendy's face fell.

"We need to think about this instead of fighting with one another." Dorothy helped Susan up and picked up the wet robe. She led Susan into her bedroom and put the soaked robe over the radiator to dry. The other girls sat on the bed and looked up at her, waiting for her to continue.

"What is the one advantage that an adult has over a child in this world?" Dorothy stood before them as if lecturing her students. "Money. Adults have money and resources. Where we've been, sandwiches grow on trees and you can find marmalade in any cupboard. But here you can't do anything without money."

Susan snapped her fingers. "I bought him a drink at a soda fountain," she said. "I don't even remember agreeing to buy it. I just followed him in and let him order. And when the bill came, he just looked at me like he expected me to get it."

"That sounds like Peter, alright." Wendy muttered. "I sewed his shadow back on and he crowed about how clever he was."

"He's probably working his way up to asking for something big," Alice said. "I wonder what, though."

"I think I know how we can find out." Dorothy said.

Dorothy and Alice crouched out of sight around the corner of Mrs. Lovett's building while Susan sat under the apple tree around front, pretending to read a book in the sunlight. Dorothy looked up to the open window of Wendy's bedroom impatiently.

"Anything yet?" She called up.

Wendy leaned out the window to look down at her. "No. But if you don't quit asking, you'll give away your hiding place." She left the window, no doubt to go stare down at Susan from the window in the other wall.

The minutes seemed to drag by. Alice crouched patiently by the corner. But Dorothy had to back away so that she could let off nervous energy. She'd never really been that good at waiting. She leaned against the brick wall of the building and picked at the flaking gold paint. Suddenly they heard a whistle from the open window above.

"That's the signal!" Alice called back as she sprang from her hiding place.

The three girls met on the sidewalk in front of the building.

Susan and the boy were about a block ahead of them on the same sidewalk. Dorothy squinted to make out his features. He stood at about the tall girl's shoulder height with sandy brown hair and green clothing. He reminded Dorothy of pictures from one of Shakespeare's plays about fairies.

"Is that Peter?" She asked Wendy.

Wendy squinted at the two people up ahead of them and then shrugged. "I don't know. It looks like it could be."

"Faster, or we'll lose them!" Alice said.

Once or twice it looked like the boy would pull Susan toward a trolley stop. But every time, Susan would back away and shake her head. Now that she was aware of whatever spell the boy weaved, she seemed immune to it. Dorothy almost laughed when she saw the boy stamp his foot in frustration the moment Susan's back was turned. Out of the corner of her eye, she saw Wendy smile at that as well.

As the morning wore on, their path meandered toward the fairground.

"The fair!" Alice slapped her forehead. "We should have guessed."

They crossed a street against traffic and rounded a corner of a building. The sounds of carnival barkers and the excited cries of children mingled with the whoosh of the wooden roller coaster and the soft melody of a pipe organ playing carnival music called to them like the sirens from a Greek epic.

"Did everyone remember their money?" Dorothy asked.

"Yes, of course." Alice said.

Just as Susan and the boy reached the entrance, she grabbed his arm and motioned for the three of them to join her.

"Looks like we're done playing pretend," Wendy said. The three of them rushed up before anyone could mistake Susan for a kidnapper. The boy flopped and thrashed like a winged monkey, but Susan had a height and weight advantage over him. When the boy realized that he was surrounded, all the fight seemed to leave him. He collapsed on the ground as if he'd been shot.

Wendy stared into his face. Then she shook her head. "It's not Peter."

"Not?" Susan stiffened. She glared down at the boy. "Then who is it?"

"I'm right here, you know," he said.

"Who are you?" Susan corrected herself.

"Why should I tell you?" He glared at them.

"Because I've got a bucket of water back in my rooms and I'm not afraid to use it!" Dorothy said.

"What are you going to do, throw it on me?" He sneered at her.

"Close," Dorothy put her hands on her hips. "I'll use the water in it to give you a bath!"

The little boy flinched. "Anything but that!"

"And then we'll wash behind your ears!" Alice added.

"And the back of your neck," Susan said.

"And under your fingernails," Wendy chimed in.

"Girls are no fun," The boy sighed. "Fine, my name is Robin Goodfellow." The girls looked at one another in confusion. "Don't any of you teach literature?" He added in an annoyed tone.

"History," Alice said. "I can tell you everything you want to know about William the Conqueror. And his mice."

"Archery," Susan said.

"Home Economics," Wendy put in. "I darn a mean sock."

Robin sighed. He cleared his throat and began reciting poetry.

"That shrewd and knavish sprite
Call'd Robin Goodfellow: are not you he
That frights the maidens of the villagery;
Skim milk, and sometimes labour in the quern
And bootless make the breathless housewife churn;
And sometime make the drink to bear no barm;
Mislead night-wanderers, laughing at their harm?
Those that Hobgoblin call you and sweet Puck,
You do their work, and they shall have good luck:
Are not you he?"

"Oh!" The four girls said at once.

"Puck! Like in Shakespere." Dorothy added. "Why didn't you say something?"

"I thought I did." Robin growled at her.

Susan crouched down so that she could look Robin in the face. She folded her arms over her knees. "What do you want with me, Robin?"

The sprite looked at her with hopeful eyes. "I need your help, Lady Susan of the Bow."

"Why didn't you ask for it to begin with?"

He looked at the four of them. "I wasn't sure you would give it. You've all been to the fairylands. And you've all come back slightly burned by the experience. I thought you might not want anything to do with any of my kind again."

The other three girls looked at Dorothy. She wondered when she became the unofficial group spokesman. "What kind of help do you need?"

"There is a portal to the fairylands here." He waved to indicate the fairgrounds. "It's located in the hot air balloon ride, so I have to pay a fee to enter the grounds. And another fee for the ticket to ride."

"You need money," Susan sounded disappointed.

"It's true." He looked down. "I am penniless. But I also cannot touch your money. The pure silver in the coins burns me."

"But it's not . . ." Alice started to say. Dorothy silenced her with a look. She turned back to Robin. "We need to have a conference."

She and the other three moved a few feet down the sidewalk and put their heads together. "Silver coins are mixed with copper," Alice said. "If it's not pure silver, he might be able to touch it."

Dorothy put her hand out so that it was level. Then she tilted it to the right and left as if weighing a scale. "Maybe, maybe not. He doesn't have to know that." She glanced over her shoulder to where Robin was examining a dandelion on the edge of the sidewalk. "I think we can buy him a ticket to fairy land, if he lets us go with him."

"What about your family, Dorothy?" Susan asked. "Don't you want to stay for them?"

She thought fleetingly of her relatives, then dismissed them. "Aunt Em and Uncle Henry are moving to San Franciso. They don't need me. It's time to let go."

The other girls looked at each other and slowly nodded as if reaching the same conclusion. They broke apart and turned to find Robin standing right behind them. "Well?" he asked.

"We'll help you." Dorothy said.

"Wonderful!" He clapped his hands together.

Dorothy held her index finger up. "On one condition. We want to go with you."

Robin looked down. He scuffed his toe in the dirt. "I can't take you back to my land. Tatiana wouldn't approve."

Dorothy turned back toward the boarding house. The other girls fell in step alongside her. "How unfortunate for you." She threw over her shoulder.

"Wait!" Robin sounded desperate. Dorothy fought the smile that threatened to break across her face. He ran around her and blocked her retreat, dancing from one foot to the other. "I can't take you where I'm going. But maybe we can find a place that would suit you."

"Don't waste my time, Goodfellow." Dorothy said in a bored voice. "I've got papers to grade."

"There are hundreds of places in fairyland." Robin blurted out. "I'm sure we can find some place. Somewhere in need of four smart, resourceful champions out to thwart evil."

Susan squeezed Dorothy's shoulder while Wendy clapped her hands.

"You have a deal, Goodfellow," she said. To the others she added: "Does anyone need to pack?"

"No," the other three girls chorused.

"Good!" Robin turned and strutted down the sidewalk toward the fair as if leading a parade.

As they followed him, Susan grabbed Dorothy's arm to stop her. "It won't be like Oz, you know."

"I know," Dorothy nodded. "But maybe it'll be better."

About the Author

Tracy is a freelance writer and photographer living in the Fort Smith area with her husband and two dogs. She is the author of the Tranquility series, of which Locus Magazine called *Bride of Tranquility* "A promising first novel." You can find her at http://www.tracysmorris.com

Kansas Sucks!

Selina Rosen

They said I'd been wandering across the barren Kansas prairie for weeks. "Auntie" Em took me to the new farm house, all the while telling me what a miracle it was that I had lived through my ordeal.

I explained about OZ and all the wonderful things I'd done and seen there, but how I was sure glad to be home. Uncle Henry and auntie Em just got these pained expressions on their faces and... Well they might as well have just gone ahead and said, "You poor, poor child," because clearly they didn't believe a word I said and thought I was an ace short of a deck.

My insistence—as auntie Em helped me undress and into a bath tub—that it was a really real place didn't help.

"I'm sure it seemed real, Dorothy," she patronized.

"Look," I said as she helped me dry off and get into one of her nightgowns. "The house was gone... and it's been weeks... and Toto and I are fine, aren't we? And my silver slippers are... well gone but that's how we got back home and I'm so happy to be home and..."

"Enough of your rambling, Dorothy Gale, we don't have time for all your talk of being in some fancy magic place. While you've been off lolly gagging around doing Lord knows what we had to build a new house. The rest of the farm is still in ruins and you'll have more than your usual set of chores to do around here. We don't have the time or the money for you to be sick. Not sick in body and certainly not sick in the head."

She tucked me into bed and that was when I remembered why I'd wanted to go over the rainbow in the first place. Auntie Em could be a real cast-iron bitch.

Of course they weren't my real aunt and uncle, just some people who took me in when I was orphaned. And don't think they didn't remind me of that plenty over the next few days. Any time I even started to complain about how hard they were working me, they reminded me that they'd been working while I'd been off having some adventure or other. Whenever I tried to tell them just exactly what adventure I'd had they said I'd made the whole Oz thing up and they didn't have time to listen to my fairy stories. It was all a lot of nonsense.

That's what they called it. My *nonsense*.

Toto lay beside me in my bed one night and I said to him, "It was a really real, real place, wasn't it Toto? We couldn't have just been wondering the prairie all this time, could we?"

He looked at me, barked in response, then turned away. I got the impression that the little son of a bitch was mocking me, so I pushed him onto the floor.

The farm was as screwed up as a two-peckered goat. The barn and hen house were in ruins; debris lay everywhere. I was expected to help clean up the huge mess, but everything just looked to me like a huge jigsaw puzzle with a bunch of pieces missing. It was hard to know where to start. Of course anytime I stopped Auntie Em or Uncle Henry were quick to tell me what I could do next.

One of my many chores was gathering the eggs. With nothing even approaching a real hen house, every day was an Easter-egg hunt. The hens were just laying all over the place, and my aunt and uncle insisted I find every last egg. I think the hens hid them in hard-to-get-at-places just to further confound me.

Late each afternoon Auntie Em would point me in one direction or another and tell me to go off and look for stuff the storm had picked up and dropped. I was to grab anything that looked the least bit useful.

As I pushed that wheel barrow along all I was really looking for were those silver slippers—the ones that could take me anywhere I wanted to go. Back to OZ, back to all my friends, away from Kansas.

The more they told me it was all in my head, and the more I remembered how much I hated Kansas and why, the more I absolutely believed that Oz was a real place. I didn't believe for a minute that it was just something my head made up. The more I told Auntie Em and Uncle Henry about it the more they looked at me like maybe it was time they got them a new orphan to help out around the farm.

Mostly my searches of the gray, colorless wasteland which is Kansas turned up either nothing at all or small items like a piece of horse tack, a broken cup, or a tattered piece of clothing. What I always looked hardest for and never found were those damn silver slippers.

One day I found a whole set of white dishes with blue flowers painted on them. Four plates, four cups, four bowls, and four saucers, all just sitting in the middle of a blue and white checked table cloth. Fine china without a chip in it—it was in fact perfect. It looked like someone had been on a picnic except I knew that wasn't the case because the table cloth was caked in red mud and the plates and dishes were all filthy.

Twisters do stuff like that. Trash the living shit out of a strong building and leave a wall full of canning jars unbroken sitting in the middle of it. They could drive pieces of glass into a hard-wood barn wall and a piece of roofing tin through a tree. Or they could pick up a table cloth and all the dishes on it as careful as you please and drop it with nothing broken in the middle of a barren field.

Twisters are terrible and magical things. Why couldn't one pick up the house I was in and drop it on a wicked witch in a wonderful, magical land called Oz?

I picked up the bundle of dishes carefully and put them into my wheel barrow and began searching the area frantically for those silver shoes. They just had to be right here where such a magical thing had happened. It made a certain sense. Those dishes were a sign of some kind. The shoes had to be close, they just *had* to be. I *needed* those shoes to prove to everyone else where I'd been and what I'd done. I needed those shoes to prove to *me* that it hadn't just all been a hallucination.

Mostly I needed those magical slippers to get the hell out of friggin' Kansas!

It was almost dark when I gave up and started home, Toto leading the way. "It was real, wasn't it Toto, wasn't it real?" The little bastard hoisted his leg and pissed on a tumble weed, which was stupid because it would just blow away in the next wind, so he hadn't marked a dam thing.

I blew away and went somewhere else. There I had made wonderful friends and proved myself. I'd had power and… Why would I ever want to come back here? I think that was when the first seeds of doubt about the existence of Oz really started. Reason had finally crept into Oz. If I'd been there I never would have wanted to come back to gray, nothing Kansas. I never would have left Oz in a million billion years, would I?

Auntie Em met me at the door. "You're late. No dinner for you, young lady."

I didn't care. If there were no silver slippers, there was no Oz and if there were no Oz, there was no hope that I'd ever left Kansas much less that I could leave it again.

"Dorothy girl what's wrong?" Henry asked.

"Nothing. I found some dishes." And if the slippers weren't there with those dishes laid out like they'd been moved by magic then they were nowhere to be found. Wasn't that the conclusion I'd come to? And no shoes meant none of it was real, didn't it?

Auntie Em went right to the wheel barrow and was so happy with my find that she gave me my dinner after all. I didn't eat much; I didn't really feel like it.

"Well they aren't mine but considering all we've lost it's about time we found something," Auntie Em said happily, as she went about cleaning the dishes. "Aren't you hungry, Dorothy?"

"Not really," I said honestly. "You really think I just made up Oz and the scarecrow and the tin woodsman, the lion and all?"

Uncle Henry looked at Auntie Em first and then back at me. "Dorothy, there are no such thing as witches or wizards or magical lands. It's fine to pretend and day dream, but... the truth is you're lucky just to be alive. I don't know where you were or what happened to you, but my guess is you were hurt and ran some fever. People dream strange things when they take sick."

I nodded. Part of me knew that made a lot more sense then I went to a magical land. But I wasn't quite ready to let go, and like most any person who believes something that they can't prove I dug my heals in and just didn't allow reason to sway me. It had felt real, and if it wasn't real then I had nothing, no hope. Where had I been all that time, and what had I done? If I hadn't been in Oz, then where was I?

So part of me knew it was a lost cause, but I doubled my effort to find those dam slippers.

Emily and Henry weren't bad people. Just hard working, honest folks with no patience at all for anything that smacked of the fanciful. In short they were absolutely the two most boring people you'd ever want to meet. They might as well have been Quakers. They quickly grew tired of my stories of Oz and asked me to keep them to myself when we were in town or at church. "Other people don't care a wit about your nonsense, Dorothy Gale," Auntie Em would remind me.

Toto was always a good listener. I wished there was some way for him to talk so I could make him tell me one way or the other where we'd been and what we'd really done. But he was just a dumb-ass dog now that we were back in Kansas. In Oz he'd at least done some really smart and brave things, now he was all about eating scraps and licking his nuts. Which, when I think about it, more or less proves there was no Oz. I mean why would my dog get stupid again?

I went a little nuts I guess, started sticking pins and needles in my head. I did it in private knowing what people would think. It would make me feel some better for awhile, but eventually I'd put way too many pins in my scalp and I guess some started to ooze infection. That's when auntie Em noticed.

"Child what's that on your head?" I tried to stop her from looking, but she jerked me close and when she saw the number of pins and needles stuck into my scalp she cried out. "My Lord in heaven! What's wrong with you, child?!"

I tried to explain as uncle Henry went to town to get the doctor.

I sat on a chair at the kitchen table as the doctor worked with tweezers pulling the pins and needles from my head and dressing the wounds with iodine—which stung like a bitch I gottah tell ya.

"Dorothy Gale, can you tell me why you did this to yourself?"

I shrugged, reluctant to tell him since he'd only think I was crazier than he already did.

"There has to be a reason."

"I can't find my silver shoes!" I yelled, driving the tweezers into my head as he was trying to pull one of the pins out. I calmed down because that hurt a lot.

"Can I speak with Dorothy alone?" the doctor asked auntie Em and Uncle Henry. Uncle Henry nodded in silence and pulled Em out of the room. "What are these Silver Slippers, Dorothy?"

"They're magic. They can get me out of here, out of Kansas, take me back to Oz."

"Why did you put pins into your head?"

"Because that's what the wizard did to the Scarecrow to make him smarter. He put pins in his head. I thought if I was smarter that I could find the silver shoes."

He was silent for a moment continuing to pull the pins from my head. Then he said, "Dorothy... Do you really believe you were in a magic land?"

I took a deep breath and let it out. "I... I thought so. I don't know any more. If I wasn't, then where was I and why did it feel so real?"

"Tell me about your dream, Dorothy."

I told him in detail. It took awhile. As I told him he finished taking the pins from my head and cleaning and doctoring my wounds. When we had both finished what we were doing he said, "Dorothy, I can see here…" He pointed to a big scar on my head under my hair. "…where you have had some head injury. My scientific guess would be that you were probably knocked out. You were most likely unconscious for a long time and when you woke up you didn't know who you were. It's a condition called amnesia. This magical land? You must have dreamt it while you were healing. Some part of you knew you had to get home, and when you did…well you remembered who you were."

"But it seemed so real, Doctor. Seemed like I was there, like I was doing all those things."

"We still don't really know why people dream, Dorothy, but some scientists are suggesting that our dreams are trying to solve problems in our real life. Maybe you need to think about what your dreams are trying to tell you. Obviously this Oz dream brought you back to Henry and Emily, to your home. Be reasonable, Dorothy, did sticking pins and needles into your head make you smarter?"

"No, and it sure feels better with them gone," I said honestly.

"Tell the truth, Dorothy, is there really a place called Oz?"

"No," I said, though I don't know whether I believed it yet or was just trying to make him happy.

As I lay in my bed the next morning trying to remember my dream and think of what it might be telling me, I could hear them talking about me. Was I really crazy? Was I ever going to be alright? How the hell had they gotten saddled with this whack job kid? Was a state institution the way to go? After all they could send me there and it wouldn't cost them anything.

I started to think, really think, about what the doctor had told me. If my dreams were trying to solve my real problems then what did my Oz dream really mean? Not that I wanted to go home. I hated it here. It just brought me here because there was no place else for me to go. In the dream I walked on that road trying to get to the emerald city. I was always walking trying to get someplace else.

There were all sorts of things that tried to stop me and what did I do? I smiled then. When I was in Oz when things got in our way we killed them.

"Dorothy Gale! Get up and milk that cow. She won't milk herself you know!"

"Coming, Auntie Em."

About the Author

Selina Rosen is the author of sixteen published novels and dozens of short stories which can be found in such anthologies as *Thieves' World*, *Witch Way to the Mall*, *Strip Mauled*, and *Fangs for the Mammories*. Her newest novel, *Black Rage*, seems at first to be a departure from her usual style, but the strong female protagonist and the character-driven plot are all Rosen.

Selina's most recently completed project is a novelization of the first *Duncan and Mallory* graphic novel that was co-written by Robert Asprin and Mel. White, tentatively entitled *Duncan and Mallory I*.

All of her novels are available as EBooks either at Baen's Universe, Kindle, or Smashwords. They are also available from Amazon.com, or autographed copies may be ordered at www.selinarosen.com, www.yarddogpress.com.

Selina owns Yard Dog Press (founded in 1995) and created their Bubbas of the Apocalypse universe.

The Monkey Queen of Oz
Sherri Dean

"*All right, you hairy little monsters.* I know you can hear me. One of you had better start talking!"

I was crouched next to a cage of monkeys and had been trying to get one of them to 'fess up about Oz for so long my legs had begun to cramp. Twenty-four chocolate brown eyes had stared at me, but the twelve faces they were attached to never made a peep in the hour I'd tried to stay hidden but still interrogate them

Maybe they didn't recognize me? It had been years since I'd seen them, years since I'd had my adventures and couldn't wait to get home. Now I was just looking for a way back. Back to Oz.

Since my return I'd been more than unhappy, unable to settle back into the grey world with its grey landscape, grey farms and grey way of living. I longed for the colorful world of Oz, where creatures and plants spoke and every day brought a new friend or problem to solve. I'd grown since then—now a young woman. The locals sometimes whispered 'that crazy Gale girl' as I passed them on the way into our tiny town. They sneered when I'd first tried to tell them what happened. Aunt Em and Uncle Henry never said a bad word but I could tell they were indulging me. The only one who knew the truth was Toto and he'd died last year of old age.

Aunt Em and Uncle Henry had gotten older too—Henry did less and less on the farm and relied more on the farm hands. Aunt Em, inwardly despairing I'd ever find a husband, given my history and questionable sanity, had insisted that I get an education. That way I'd be able to support myself as a teacher or governess when the day came that they'd no longer be able to. She had also been the one to suggest we travel north early spring of 1853 to witness the incorporation of Kansas City as an official city.

Kansas City did not quite compare to the color and beauty of the great Emerald City of Oz but it had a good running start. All manner of people had turned out for the dedication, from politicians with starched shirts to farming families like my own, wearing their faded but Sunday best. There were street vendors and the evening festivities promised a circus and fireworks show.

I was especially excited about the circus—the "Wonderful Wizard" of Oz, formerly of Omaha, had preceded my departure from Oz by several days and I knew he'd wanted to go back to being a balloonist for the circus again upon his return. If I could find him, if he was here maybe he'd have a way to send me back to Oz.

As Aunt Em and Uncle Henry watched two politicians debate the virtues and vices of owning slaves in Kansas (I'd seen people enslaved in Oz and my uncle shared my opinion of such a cruel practice here) my gaze wandered. From the corner of my eye I saw a red flash of silk, a balloon slowly rising at the end of the commons. My breath caught in my breast—could it be? Was it him? I tugged on Uncle Henry's sleeve and he silently dismissed me with a shoo-fly wave. I scootched out of the throng of people and took off down the street.

I followed the balloon to an odd looking clapboard construction, all light wood and shiny hinges and garish paintings. It appeared to be a flat front theatre, all fancy frosting on the outside and humble hoe cake below. There was no end to the frills and painted cherubs holding flutes and flowers.

A large sign next to the false front informed visitors of the next show time, as well as attractions that could be viewed beforehand, such as exotic animals and the Congress of Nature's Oddities. This sounded like what the old 'wizard' had spoken about and I just knew he'd be here. I grasped the handle and with a slight click the door opened and I entered.

I'd just begun walking the maze of canvas tents when I saw my first denizen of the circus. It was a tiny man, so small at first I'd thought him to be one of the performer's children, possibly playing hookey from school or practice. When he pulled a cigar from his dainty waistcoat pocket, struck a match and started puffing I realized this was not a child but a tiny man, much like the Munchkins I first encountered in Oz. He turned to stare at me, and lingered to the point of being rude before he spoke.

"What are you doing back here, young lady? The show doesn't start for another few hours."

I was surprised by the strength of his voice, slightly tinny with an echoing boom, as if used to shouting commands at great distance. I tried to match the surety of his voice in reply." I'm just looking for someone, actually, a friend I haven't seen in quite some time."

"What makes you think he's here?'

"He flies balloons for promotions of circuses and county fairs. Like the big red one over there," I pointed "I saw the storefront and thought I'd take a chance."

"Young ladies shouldn't take chances. Never know what could happen to a pretty thing as yourself. You might just... disappear. Take some advice from Mr. Large," as he thumbed at his lapel, his voice dropped, as low as his tenor could manage, and icy cold to boot. "I think you should go."

Feeling uneasy, I took a few steps back before I spun on my heel and hurried away. This 'Mr. Large,' as he called himself, looked like a Munchkin but he sure didn't act like one. Once he was out of sight I changed directions and slipped around a canvas covered corner and found myself among the wild animal cages.

The animals were mostly quiet, with the occasional snuffling of the air or raised head to stare as I walked past. I could identify most of the creatures from my study days at school, although a few I couldn't name. I moved slowly so as not to spook them as I passed and looked cautiously in each steel barred prison. There was a corral of ponies, several long-legged ostriches, giraffes and zebras. Two large elephants, each bearing a leg chain hammered into the ground, lay in the dust and flicked away gnats with their leathery ears. A sad, grizzled old lion stared from behind bars at me and I felt pity for him and all the others that were trapped here. Even if I didn't find the 'Wizard' I would find a way to help these poor beasts.

As I made my way to the end of the row I saw a large, high ceilinged cage, like a giant aviary for the world's largest parakeet. But there were no birds inside—there were monkeys.

Monkeys with wings.

My hands fluttered up in surprise and excitement, one to my throat in shock, the other to cover my mouth to prevent the scream that was building from popping out and alerting any circus folk. My thoughts swirled, I was delighted to see my friends the monkeys, at the thought of real live proof of my time in Oz. I also felt sadness at seeing such free spirited creatures in the oversize bird cage and the shabby way they lived.

When I first encountered the monkeys in Oz they terrified me, doing the bidding of the Wicked Witch of the West by capturing, and in some cases, torturing or disassembliing our little band of wayfarers. After the witch's death I'd found a funny little golden cap in one of her old cupboards and was surprised to find it could summon and control the winged monkeys. They were happy the witch was dead and were very apologetic and gracious and I used the cap the three times allowed. I then gave the cap to Glinda, good witch of the South. She too used the cap well and wisely and when done gave it to the King of the Monkeys so they would be free of the slavery of the cap. I couldn't imagine how they'd wound up in Kansas, trapped in a cage.

I stood next to the bars and whispered to the monkeys, but they seemed not to hear me. They paced or made short hops to little perches in the cage higher up, or jumped to ropes higher still. They milled about in agitation and glanced furtively. Perhaps they were trying to tell me something? I decided to go around to the back of the cage, closer to it but out of plain sight for anyone coming through the area. I tried to tuck my dress under me and kneel down without getting dirty and succeeded in plunking flat on my fundament. Oh, well- in for a penny, in for a pound.

While I re-arranged my skirt folds I heard two voices coming close to the cage. I froze and held my breath, hoping I wouldn't be seen.

"You know how he gets, Little. We don't want him upset or it'll be giant dust storms all over again!" said a voice I recognized as the unfortunately named Mr. Large. He and a mountain of a man were passing so close I could have reached out and touched their shoes, had I been stupid enough to do so.

"I know. But we've gone over the place a dozen times looking for this girl. How could a girl hurt him?" Mr. Little. "He's got the travel suit on and all the talismans. I thought he was unstoppable."

"That's a trap his sister from the West fell into. Never trust the one who looks innocent and helpless. Enough jawflapping, we've got to find her," said Mr. Large. They continued to stomp through the animal yards.

Sister from the West? Could he really mean the Wicked Witch? I hadn't meant to kill her, but it had happened thanks to a bucket of wash water. I wasn't going to let her kill me then and I certainly did not intend for them to do it now. I had to get more information. I leaned closer to the monkeys, begging "Please, fellas, I could really use your help right now."

One monkey slid down from a higher perch and made a single hoot sound, to the others higher up. He leaned in toward me, a tired look on his furry face. He pursed his lips and uttered one word: "Poot!" then laughed.

When the chuckling from the others died down the older monkey spoke. "I must apologize, but we had to make certain of two things. One, that the coast was clear, and two that you were who we presumed you to be."

"You rascals." I sighed.

He spoke again. "Listen sharp for we don't have much time. In the years since you left Oz there have been many changes. Your friends were ruling in their respective lands and things were peaceful between the four corners. But one day a sinister dust storm hit the Emerald City and at its center was a terrible being, a not quite human man that called himself the Great Humbug. The Humbug was an evil wizard, brother to the West and East Witches and mad with grief that they'd been killed, even though they were the ones who had had him exiled to the edges of the Great Desert. He was bent on finding and punishing you, Dorothy."

"His first act was to gather talismans from the leaders of Oz. From the Scarecrow he took the silver pins that made him a sharp thinker. From the Woodsman he took the golden ax handle made by the Winkies of the West. He took the Lion's golden collar, red silk from Glinda and even the crown from my father, making the monkeys slaves again. All these, together with some magical shoes …"

I gasped "My silver slippers! They fell off in the desert when I returned home!"

"…from the East and he was able to travel back and forth from Oz to your civilized country as he pleased. He found he could cloak his evildoing on your world by running a circus, as nothing would be considered out of the ordinary. He tried to bring across others, like the Kalidas, but they did not survive the journey. The only munchkin that lived you've already met in the form of Mr. Large, and the man known as Little was once a Hammerhead whose form was affected by the journey here. Even we monkeys are not supposed to be here, yet here we are through no doing of our own. The Humbug sets us loose every night to steal from the townspeople wherever we go, or he kills us. He shoots us with his gun. That's what happened to my father, your friend, the king of the monkeys."

"I'm so sorry" I said. "This is too terrible. How can we fix this?"

"Well, the Humbug wears or carries all the talismans with him. If we can destroy him then you can use them to get us all back to Oz. Once the talismans are in country things should be set right again." said the Monkey. "My name is Lolo, and you have my people at your disposal, even without the cap. It doesn't work here anyway, but bullets do. That's what has kept my people in line since we came here."

"All right Lolo, here's what we'll do."

Dusk was beginning to fall. I went to each animal cage and prayed I was doing the right thing as I opened every one. At first the animals were uncertain about their freedom. The hardest ones to free were the elephants. I didn't have the key to unlock their chains, so I used an axe that had been near a small woodpile and chopped at the chains, trying to get them as short as I could without hurting them. They both nuzzled me with their trunks as I chopped, as if to hurry me along. With the final chop they turned to look past me and stopped. I turned to look too and was surprised to see Little and Large running at me full bore. The elephants didn't hesitate, but gently brushed past me and loomed over the tiny Mr. Large. He swore at them and kicked one with his miniscule foot, which only served to annoy it. The bigger elephant then circled Large's waist in his trunk and picked him right up off the ground, then swung him like a mallet towards Mr. Little who was busy trying to beat the other elephant with a stick of firewood. While Little was being beaten with Large I scurried like a mouse to the monkeys.

I used the ax again to chop the lock off the monkey's cage and held open the low door so they could swoop out. The wind gusted past with each flapping of their great wings. Lolo and another monkey picked me up and together we flew in search of the Great Humbug. As we passed over the grounds I saw people chasing the animals, most of whom had the good fortune to escape. I wondered what Aunt Em would think if she came to gather eggs from the henhouse and found an ostrich there, or if Uncle Henry would try to tame a zebra and train it to pull a plow.

The red balloon was getting closer. I'd gathered that this, plus the travel suit of the Humbug, would be our way back to Oz. Twelve monkeys and I riding together would be a tight fit but I had to get back to put things right again. We scanned the grounds below until we saw a man with a bright red coat and a black top hat, a man who wasn't human looking at all. Steam billowed from what looked like nostrils, and a great gnashing of his teeth could be heard. He bellowed orders that no one obeyed. His empire was falling, he was angry and afraid.

Lolo and the other monkey set me down gently on the ground near, but not too near, the Humbug. I looked him right in his red eyes and felt a calm fall over me. After all, I'd beaten two witches before and survived the trip across the Great Desert—I was strong enough to do this for my friends.

The Humbug pounced on me at once. I fell to the ground, taking him with me. In the fall I saw that he dropped his gun, the one the monkeys were so afraid of. I rolled away, swept in with one leg and kicked the gun away, out of reach. A nearby ostrich stared at it with a quizzical look, then promptly ate it.

"Dorothy! Stand back!" Lolo yelled.

I jumped away from the Humbug and the monkeys swarmed him. I had once seen locusts strip a field bare in no time flat and the monkeys did the same. The Humbug's screams were terrible but short lived and when the monkeys were done they brought me his coat with the talismans and the golden ax handle he'd been using as a walking stick. Last to be recovered were the silver shoes, which I had to rinse off before donning as the monkeys had gotten them bloody in the frenzy. As I dried, then slipped them on I felt a tingling sensation, as if they'd waited for me to wear them once more.

Monkeys are not fond of water, but they did wash out the gore from their coats when I asked politely. As the last of the monkeys dried off, I saw Aunt Em and Uncle Henry round the corner and stop, staring at me.

"Dorothy, we were so frightened! We didn't know where you were!" cried Em. She hugged me, and then they both stared at the monkeys. I fidgeted.

"This is Lolo. He's the King of the Flying Monkeys." I said. Lolo, on his best behavior and sensing he should remain mum, bowed low to Em and Henry. "I'm going to return to Oz. My friends there need my help."

"Well, I suspected it might come to this someday." said Henry. "You've never really been happy since you've been home. Does this mean we'll never see you again?"

"I don't know how long they'll need me. But I'll miss you always."

They helped me get into the balloon and the monkeys quickly followed. As the balloon lifted off and we began to gently float away Lolo turned to me and asked "When we get back to Oz would you consider being our queen? With the silver slippers you can do anything in Oz, and we monkeys seem unable to hold our crown. We'd rather you have it and be our benevolent ruler. Would you?"

Twenty four chocolate brown eyes stared at me from twelve furry faces.

And just like that, I became the Monkey Queen of Oz.

About the Author

Sherri Dean was born both late AND backwards in a small town in Missouri—which explains a lot. Her mundane hours are spent as a veteran of the animal health field (and the recipient of many a puppy piddling) until she gets rich and famous. Or was that infamous? She spends her quality time writing, illustrating, making crazy costumes and reading comics.

She credits Forrest J "Uncle Forry" Ackerman for her love of Science Fiction, fantasy and horror, and is active in genre conventions throughout the Midwest. It is at one of these early conventions she encountered the infamous Selina "Buy My Books!" Rosen and was thusly corrupted (Ah, but who corrupted whom?) to submit artwork, stories and mad editing skills for Yard Dog Press. Sherri also works hard to fulfill her role as Ms Rosen's 'straight man' in comedy. (She's a giver, folks! That's what she does!)

Sherri has long referred to herself in the third person, the 'royal we' if you will, as the Queen of the Flying Monkeys for years and is only now letting the public in on her secret. (If you've met her you already know. If not, do so and BUY HER STUFF from Yard Dog Press) In addition to commanding her monkey minions, she likes shiny presents, donuts and hearing from fans on Facebook. Now, get thee to a computer and make with the monkey adoration!

WHO RODE THE WINDS
Bradley H. Sinor and Susan P. Sinor

Nathan Grayson was humming "Rule Britannia" when Dorothy came into the room. He didn't see her, which irritated Dorothy no end. After all, they were not only *not* supposed to be here, Nathan was in the process of committing a crime by opening a wall safe that did not belong to him. Not to mention the fact that he was severely off key. From past experience, that was a good sign; it meant he was close to finishing.

"You realize I could hear you halfway down the hall," she said quietly.

Nathan stopped what he was doing and looked at Dorothy. "Bring the light over here."

Dorothy rolled her eyes; Nathan was only two years younger than she, but sometimes he acted like he was still around fourteen, complete with the cocksure arrogance of someone that age. There were definitely moments, like this one, that she wanted to take a two by four to him.

"You were also supposed to have been done fifteen minutes ago," she said, and picked up a lamp, setting it on the table close to Nathan.

"Relax, my dear Miss Gale, you cannot hurry true artistry, and I, Madam, am an artist."

Nathan plastered his ear to the metal door of the safe and began to work the dial.

Outside the window the lights that illuminated the grounds seemed to have grown brighter. Dorothy suspected it was only her eyes growing more accustomed to the dim light inside the house.

Since Jay Gatsby had come to West Egg, Long Island, he had thrown parties every weekend, with several hundred people circulating among the tents set up on his lawn. Doing something like this in the middle of a crowd wasn't their ordinary type of job. Nathan's and Dorothy's usual forte was empty apartments, office safes, and even the occasional bit of corporate espionage.

However, finding a box, apparently appearing out of nowhere, on her kitchen table had gotten Dorothy's attention. Inside had been information about Gatsby, his parties, invitations dated for the next Saturday, and the location of the safe. How it had gotten there she didn't know, and that scared Dorothy, since, outside of Nathan, there were not more than a half dozen people who knew what she did for a living.

This whole thing seemed like an elaborate practical joke on someone's part. Of course, if it was a joke, it was an awfully expensive one, since there had been five hundred dollars, in non sequential bills, included with the instructions. The money, which now resided in her safety deposit box, was a good argument for the job being on the up and up.

"What the hell," said Nathan. "I don't have a date Saturday, so we might as well earn the money."

There was a sharp click and Nathan yanked down on the handle of the wall safe. Dorothy didn't have to look at him to know that he had a large grin on his face. Nathan stood up without even looking at the safe and walked over to a small table near the window where he poured two fingers of an amber colored liquid into a cut glass tumbler.

She pulled open the safe door and looked inside. Their instructions had said that they "would know what it was when they saw it."

There was a small pile of papers in the safe, along with several boxes, not to mention bundles of cash. The problem was, there was nothing in front of her that said *"Take me."* Dorothy found a package pushed to the back, pulled it out and began to unwrap it.

"Find something?" asked Nathan.

"Don't know," muttered Dorothy. "It feels like a shoe."

Pulling the last of the paper away, Dorothy could see it was a silver slipper. She stared at it for a moment, then collapsed unconscious on the floor.

"What happened?" Dorothy's voice was raspy and, if she hadn't known what she had said, she wouldn't have understood herself.

"Very original," Nathan said, helping her to sit up. "You fainted."

Dorothy hated those mealy-mouthed girls who would get the vapors, as her grandmother had called it, and pass out at the drop of a hat. Those were the ones who seemed to think they could run the world by just fluttering their eyelashes

That was when she realized the silver slipper was still in her hand. Everything became fuzzy again and she felt herself starting to slump backward.

A blonde-haired man, in a well pressed tuxedo, came bursting out of the shadows and pushed Nathan aside to grab Dorothy by the shoulders.

"There's some brandy by the chair; bring it!" the man told Nathan. His voice had a tone that said he was used to being obeyed. Nathan looked around nervously, then returned with a half-full snifter that he gave the man.

The liquid was warm as it rolled down Dorothy's throat. She looked down at the slipper. It seemed a normal pump, but the surface was silver and reflected even the tiniest bit of light.

"Who are you?" Nathan said from behind the man.

"Actually, I'm the one who should be asking you this question, old sport. Gatsby's the name. Jay Gatsby. And you are?"

Dorothy could see the color drain out of Nathan's face. Finding yourself face to face with the person that you were attempting to rob was not something you plan for.

"Nathan Grayson. I hardly expected to see you here tonight, Mr. Gatsby. Nice party," he said.

"Thanks, I don't usually go to them, myself," Gatsby said. "I was in here when you arrived, so I decided to watch."

"I usually don't work with an audience," muttered Nathan.

Dorothy ignored the two men for a moment, looking down at the silver shoe. It fascinated her; it was beautiful and familiar and yet there was something frightening about it.

"This shoe," she said. "I think that it's what we were sent here for."

"Now, that's interesting, young lady. But let's get you up off the floor," said Gatsby.

Nathan pulled a leather chair over while Gatsby helped Dorothy stand. She was steadier on her feet, though she grabbed onto the edge of the desk for support. She didn't actually need it, but it never hurt to give the impression you were less than you were.

Gatsby went behind his desk, stopping to stare out the window at the crowd of partiers. For a moment there was a faraway look in his eyes, which disappeared almost immediately

"So you were sent here to steal that shoe. Why?" he asked. "By the way, we haven't been formally introduced."

Dorothy smiled. She considered for a moment giving a phony

name. The driver's license in her purse identified her as Eliza Santee, but there was something about this man that suggested he would recognize a lie when he heard it.

"Gale. Dorothy Gale."

Gatsby stared at her for a minute, then reached into his pocket and pulled out a ring of keys. Selecting an odd green-colored one, he used it to unlock a drawer in his desk. He brought out several photos that he handed to Dorothy.

She looked at them and felt the bottom fall out of her stomach. Images rolled through her head, faces that she had long ago pushed back in the recess of her mind as dreams, nightmares and things that couldn't be.

Nathan stepped up to the desk and looked at the photos spread out in front of his friend. The first photo was rather blurry, just a figure with some kind of bird hovering above it. He had to look at it for several seconds before realizing that the bird looked like it had arms and what might have been a tail. He picked up the other two pictures and saw the same thing, but with two more of the creatures in them, baring their teeth like they had been captured in mid snarl.

"What the hell are these things?"

"Flying monkeys, the most vicious, nasty creatures you can imagine. In a herd they can make piranha look like goldfish," said Dorothy. "But they're not real, just the nightmares of a poor sick little girl who lost her family and her mind in a tornado."

"Actually, Miss Gale, those creatures are all too real," said Gatsby. "And those nightmares of yours, well they were real, too."

Dorothy felt herself on the verge of tears, but pushed those feelings back, refusing to show them to Gatsby, Nathan or herself. This whole evening had turned into some totally bent version of reality. Part of her wished she had burned that damn package the moment she found it on her kitchen table, but another part of her, the little girl who watched her world disintegrate in the whirling chaos of the twister, was grasping for something that said the dreams had been real.

"Oz? It was real?"

"Oz," echoed Nathan. "Wasn't there some sort of book or something called that?"

"Yes. A best-seller, as a matter of fact, as-well-as a Broadway musical not to mention a couple of movies. All of that thanks to a nosy reporter named Baum getting his hands on part of Miss Gale's case file. He got a lot of the story right, but a lot wrong, as well. Those sequels were total balderdash."

"Wait a minute," Dorothy said. "You're trying to tell me that it was real; Oz, the tin woodsman, the scarecrow, the wicked witch. That, it wasn't a nightmare after Auntie Em and Uncle Henry were killed when the tornado hit the house," she said. "No. No, the doctors told me over and over again it was just a dream."

"But dreams sometimes do come true," Gatsby said gently. "We needed you to believe that it was a dream. That was the only way to protect the place. That's what a lot of us have done for a very long time. We weren't certain that you, at that age, could keep secret the idea that the place was real."

"I became involved because one of the men in the company I commanded during the war was dying and felt like he had to tell someone," said Gatsby.

"Then what are we doing here? Why do you have the shoe?" said Dorothy. She still wasn't sure if she believed him, but pushing ahead and asking questions would keep her from dwelling on it and those long cold years where the doctors kept telling her it had all been a dream.

"I've been holding the shoe for its proper owner. It looks like that's you. Otherwise, it wouldn't have glowed when you touched it," he said. "As for who sent you here, I suspect that your answer lies in Omaha, Nebraska," said Gatsby.

"Nebraska," said Nathan. "Hasn't that place dulled away by now?"

"Dorothy, you need to go there to see Oscar Zoroaster Phadrig Isaac Norman Henkel Emmanuel Ambrose Diggs," said Gatsby.

"Who?" said Dorothy.

"My dear Miss Dorothy Gale, you're off to see the Wizard, the Wizard of Oz."

"Didn't I play this scene before?" Dorothy Gale asked herself.

"What scene?" asked Nathan as he paced back and forth on the sidewalk. Omaha, Nebraska was not the smallest town in the world; there were several that Dorothy remembered from Kansas where the entire town would fit on the street outside the train station.

"Going off to see the Wizard, except that wasn't a yellow brick road we just spent far too many hours on," she said.

"So are you remembering that stuff that Gatsby was talking about?" asked Nathan.

"I never forgot it; really. Those doctors drugged me up enough that I believed that it was really just one long nightmare," she said. "It's just hard now accepting the fact the whole thing was actually real. Do you see a telephone booth anywhere?"

They walked a half block away from the train station before spotting a phone booth. The phone directory was small, made of pulp paper, and the pages were stained and torn from too much handling and being out in the weather.

She paged through the book to the Ds and ran her finger down the listings. "Hm, nobody named Diggs. Do you think he could have moved?"

"I doubt it," Nathan said. "Gatsby wouldn't have sent us here if he had. Look in the commercial listings, maybe under entertainment. He's supposed to be a wizard."

Dorothy paged to that section, surprised to see how big it was for a town this size. For a moment it seemed like this was another dead end. Then she saw it: Oz the Great – Stage Magician – reasonable rates. Call 359.

"Well, call 359," Nathan told her, reaching into his pocket. "Here's a nickel."

Dorothy hesitated. "Do you think he can really help us...me?"

"Call him; then we'll know." Nathan reached into the booth and put the nickel in the slot. "Call."

Dorothy gave the number to the operator; when no one answered, she admitted to herself that she felt relieved. At least for awhile she wouldn't have to look into the face of the unknown.

"I don't know about you," said Nathan. "I noticed a diner down the street. What do you say to a couple of blue plate specials?"

"I think that would be an excellent idea for all three of us. I could use a bit of sustenance myself."

Dorothy and Nathan turned to find themselves facing a rather portly man with a large nose, wearing a top hat, with a green watch chain coming out of his vest pocket. He looked a lot like a vaudeville comedian named Fields that she had seen perform a few weeks before.

"Were you speaking to us?" said Nathan.

"Indeed I was, young man," said the newcomer. "Miss Gale, I believe?"

Dorothy and Nathan looked at each other, then at the stranger. "Who might be asking?" Dorothy said to him, though she had a feeling that this was not the first time she had laid eyes on the man.

"I am Professor Oscar Zoroaster Phadrig Isaac Norman Henkel Emmannuel Ambrose Diggs; Oz Diggs." He said with a flourish.

"I remember you," said Dorothy "You're the Wizard!"

"The very same," the man said. With that, Dorothy slapped him, the sound a crack that could be heard above the west wind that had picked up in the last few minutes.

"How could you let them treat me like that? Make me think that I was crazy," she said, her voice halfway between anger and tears.

"I'm sorry, Dorothy. It was for your own good. Better a few years of thinking that you dreamed it all than decades in a lunatic asylum," he said gently.

"It was also to protect Oz itself, the fewer people who know, the better."

"Professor," said Nathan. "Why don't we get something to eat and talk there."

"Young man, you are exactly right."

"We'll have three blue plate specials," Professor Diggs said to the waitress. "Put it on my tab."

They had taken a booth at the far end of the diner, several tables away from the establishment's few other patrons. Dorothy continued to stare at the man who called himself Oz. Memories that she had locked away came flooding back, events, impressions, sights, smells.

"How was your journey from West Egg?" said the professor

"How do you know where we came from?" asked Nathan.

"Oh, I know many things: where you came from, where you're going."

"*We* don't know where we're going; how can you know that?" asked Dorothy.

Just then their meal arrived. They ate for a few minutes before Diggs spoke. "Perhaps I should start from the beginning, Miss Gale. May I call you Dorothy? First let me apologize for the things that my colleagues and I put you through when you returned from Oz. It was necessary to protect that wonderful place."

"Indeed, there are not many of us who know of its reality; Gatsby, myself and a few others, but those of us who do try to protect it. You can imagine what people would do if they knew a 'magic' land existed."

"How well do you know Gatsby?"

"Oh, I've known him for years, since he lived in this part of the country. A really nice young man, although I can't say I approve of his business interests, but we all have our crosses to bear," said the wizard.

"And no one has found proof, after all these years?" said Dorothy.

"Not many. The books and the movies and that play only helped make everyone think it was nothing more than a fantasy story. We did have a problem with a young archeology student named Jones a year or two ago, but we diverted his attention into other areas," said Diggs between bites. "What few artifacts find their way here are kept hidden."

"Like that silver slipper," said Nathan.

"Indeed, it was the power of the silver slippers that returned Dorothy to this world. Dorothy, my dear, touching that shoe brought back all the reality of your time in Oz. I understand how painful that has been, but it was necessary," said Diggs.

"Necessary?" Dorothy asked. She had always been hesitant when someone told her something was necessary. There were too many memories connected to that word, memories leading back to her time in the "doctor's care."

"We need your help in protecting Oz from a very great danger," said Diggs; his friendly face had gone hard. Under the right circumstances, it was an expression that might have sent chills up someone's spine.

"And that would be?" asked Nathan.

"Both the best thing and the worst thing to ever happen to the land of Oz. I am referring to L. Frank Baum."

Nathan pursed his lips for a moment, as if struggling to remember something. 'Wait a minute," he finally said. "I think I remember something about this Baum fellow dying a few years ago."

Professor Diggs paused to take a sip of his coffee.

"Indeed he did. In fact, Baum was a good man who stumbled on the whole Oz matter by pure accident. He amassed quite a collection of Oz memorabilia, including a few things that actually came from Oz."

"Am I right in guessing he has the other silver slipper, since we only have one of them?" said Dorothy

"Exactly. It was their magic that returned you from Oz. They can take someone back. In the wrong hands that would be a disaster," said the old stage magician.

"True, but his son, Frank Joslyn Baum, has gone into business with a Captain Hugh Fitzgerald, who has taken over the memorabilia collection and knows that Oz exists," said the professor.

"And you need someone to steal that silver slipper," Nathan said.

Dorothy smiled and looked over at Nathan. He had always been sharp and adaptable, willing to work with any situation. That had been one of the things that had attracted her to him.

"So I had to find out if you were as good as your reputation suggested before I pulled you into our little project. That's why I sent you the information on Gatsby's safe. I needed to know if you were good enough. It was a test and you passed with flying colors," he said.

"So how do we find this silver slipper that the good Captain has?" asked Nathan

"One slipper will always know where the other is," said Diggs.

"Does this mean we have to go back to West Egg and get Gatsby's slipper?"

The wizard smiled and shook his head. He gestured at Dorothy's purse sitting on the seat next to her. Without a word she opened the bag, pulling out her compact, wallet and key ring. When she looked back in her purse, the silver slipper was there.

"Nicely done, sir," she said, pulling out the slipper with two fingers. The feel of the material in her hands left them tingling. She remembered the feel of them on her feet, the way the sensation had spread up through her when she had clicked the heels together and thought of being 'home'.

"It was there all along, just a spell that made no one notice it until I took it off. It's not something I can do very often anymore. I'm not as young as I used to be. But it is very handy. I have to save my strength for bigger things." he said.

"All right, Oh Great and Mighty Oz. Give me one good reason that Nathan and I should do this little job that you're asking us to do."

Professor Oscar Zoroaster Phadrig Isaac Norman Henkel Emmanuel Ambrose Diggs picked up his coffee cup and took a sip. For a moment he had a vague distant, almost sad, look in his eyes.

"I'm not asking you to do it for me, for Gatsby or for any of the others that you haven't met. I'm asking you to do it for that little girl, scared out of her wits, who rode the winds into a land of dreams and wonder."

They were all three silent for a time, then Dorothy picked up the slipper and put it back in her bag. "When's the next train?" she asked the Wizard.

"There I think I can help you out a little bit," said the wizard as he pulled an envelope from inside his jacket and passed it over to his younger companions. "That will fill you in on Captain Hugh Fitzgerald. Now, I need you to just go through that door over on the left."

The door that Diggs referred to had the word Storage stenciled on it. Dorothy looked at him oddly and saw the same twinkle in his eyes that she remembered from the first time in the throne room in The Emerald City.

"Go on, my dear," he said gently.

I thought you said this guy was a stage magician, a fake," said Nathan.

The door that the wizard had directed them through had led down a short corridor and out onto the street, only it wasn't a street in Omaha.

They were standing near the Busy Bee Dry Goods store; just down the street she could see a grove of several dozen trees covered with what looked like oranges. Looking back toward the door the two of them had come through, Dorothy saw nothing but a wooden wall covered with advertising posters.

"I guess I was wrong," Dorothy replied. "Do you have that envelope he gave us?"

Nathan paused for a minute, patting his pockets, and Dorothy didn't like the look she saw on his face, he did have a tendency to lose things.

"Bingo," he proclaimed pulling the papers from his inside coat packet, along with several other scraps of paper and a leather case that she knew was his picklock set.

"Okay, let's see what the professor has in mind," she said unfolding two typewritten sheets. "It looks like we're in Hollywood, California. I wonder if we'll run into Charlie Chaplin?"

"Coming out of Busy Bee Dry Goods? Hardly," said Nathan.

Nathan disappeared into that same store. Two minutes later he was back out on the street smiling "This Fitzgerald fellow's address is number 22 Orange Drive. Although, apparently, Captain Fitzgerald won't be home tonight; he's attending a party at Pickfair."

"Pickfair? As in...." said Dorothy.

"Mary Pickford and Douglas Fairbanks place. If we had time, I wouldn't mind crashing that little shindig."

It took them nearly an hour to find the house. By that time the sun was sinking into the west. Even though she couldn't actually see the ocean from where they were, Dorothy stopped for a moment to look in that direction. Growing up in Kansas, the ocean would have seemed as far away as Oz, and now here she was, only a few miles from it.

On the far side of the property they slipped over the fence and made it up to the house without encountering anyone. Nathan saw a basement window and had it open and was through it in only a matter of minutes.

"Your turn," Nathan called out to her, reaching up to grab her as she wiggled through the narrow space.

"We're in; now what?"

Dorothy remembered the words of the Great and Powerful Oz, "one slipper will always know where the other is."

"I suppose we could ask the slipper," she said.

The fact that she hadn't thought about the silver slipper since their last moment in Omaha bothered Dorothy, but not much. Magic just seemed to have stepped back into her life like it had never left.

Her hand tingled as she held the slipper. Walking up the staircase, the sensation increased as they moved into the main part of the house.

"So where are we going?" asked Nathan.

"We're following the yellow brick road." Dorothy gestured at the floor where a long winding yellow strip had been painted. The slipper was also leading them along the same path. She felt an odd sensation of déjà vu following it right up to a large door painted with the royal crest of OZ.

"Dis must be the place," Nathan said.

The door wasn't locked, though the hinges groaned loudly as they opened it. If there was anyone else in the house, that surely would have alerted them that something was going on.

"Don't turn any lights on," she muttered.

The room was filled to overflowing with OZ memorabilia: props, books, advertising posters. Dorothy paused in front of the hat that had belonged to the Wicked Witch of the West in one of the movies and felt like she could still hear that evil woman's cackling laugh; the memory was frightening, yet oddly reassuring.

From the other side there was a sudden flapping noise followed by a crash as Nathan fell. Dorothy turned and saw her partner on the floor, his hands flailing at something.

Running to his side, she saw there was an animal of some kind on Nathan's chest, pawing at his face. Thinking it was a cat, she grabbed for the scruff of creatures neck and jerked backwards. Only, this was no cat; it took a few seconds for her to realize she was holding a small monkey with wings! Her stomach twisted in fear, and she fought down an urge to scream and run away. Then just as quickly, she slammed her fist into the creature's stomach; it slumped and went limp.

"What the hell is that?" said Nathan as he struggled to his feet.

Before Dorothy could say the words 'flying monkey' she heard the sound of footsteps in the hallway outside the room. She grabbed a heavy green cabinet and began pushed it up against the door.

From outside the door came a voice. "I tell you I heard something in there! It sounded like all hell was breaking loose."

Something pounded hard against the door, but the barrier held, although Dorothy had her doubts for how long.

"Get Dorkins; we'll break the door down and then send someone for the police," said a second voice.

"Nathan, we need to get out of here now," she said, looking around.

The problem was, there were no windows. Every inch of the walls were covered by display cases, bookshelves or framed posters. As best Dorothy could guess, this room was in the center of the house, so that left only one exit, the main door.

"Maybe there's a secret panel or a tunnel of some sort?" said Nathan.

Just then Dorothy spotted the silver slipper lying on the ground where she had dropped it going to Nathan's rescue. Instinctively, she grabbed it up. As soon as her hand touched the slipper, it tingled like it never had before.

In the middle of the broken remnants of the display case that Nathan had fallen into, Dorothy caught a glimpse of something silver. Frantically, she began to push shattered pieces of wood and glass aside. Its content was a single shoe, a silver slipper. Dorothy grabbed it up, a warm feeling running through her as held them.

The pounding on the door began again and, without thinking about it, Dorothy pulled her shoes off and replaced them with the silver slippers.

"I'm open for suggestions on how to get out of here," said Nathan as the pounding on the door increased.

Dorothy reached over and took his hand. "Just believe," she said, then touched the heels of her slippers together. "The last time I did this I ended up back in Kansas."

Exactly what happened next was unclear to Dorothy. Everything seemed to whirl around her, and, for one terrifying moment, she was back in the tornado that long ago day in Kansas. Then she and Nathan came crashing to the ground, rolling over and over until they stopped. Dorothy opened her eyes and looked around. She and Nathan were lying in a field of the most beautiful flowers she had ever seen. Around the field were stately trees bearing rich fruit. She felt her breath come in gasps for a moment. She knew this place; it was Munchkinland in Oz.

"That hurt," Nathan groaned, as he looked around. "You said the last time you used those shoes you ended up in Kansas. Well, I don't think I'm wrong when I say, we're not in Kansas."

About the Authors

Bradley H. Sinor has seen his work appear in numerous science fiction, fantasy and horror anthologies such as *The Improbable Adventures Of Sherlock Holmes*, *Tales Of The Shadowmen*, *The Grantville Gazette* and *Ring Of Fire 2 And 3*. Three collections of his short fiction have been released by Yard Dog Press, *Dark And Stormy Nights*, *In The Shadows*, and *Playing With Secrets* (along with stories by his wife Sue Sinor.) His newest collections are *Echoes From The Darkness* (Arctic Wolf Press) and *Where The Shadows Began* (Merry Blacksmith Press).

Susan (Sue) Sinor writes short stories, mostly urban fantasy, which have been published in various anthologies, including Yard Dog Press's *Bubbas of the Apocalypse* anthologies. She also has collaborated with her husband, Bradley H. Sinor, on several stories. They live in Tulsa, OK, where they are the housekeeping staff for two cats.

But Wait, There's More!
Allison Stein

Ladies and gentlemen,
- Are you feeling as if your head is stuffed full of straw?
- Have you lost all heart for things, people, and activities that used to fill you with joy and passion?
- Does the mere thought of confronting your problems and the people who cause them leave you cowering in a corner?
- Has your most cherished loved one become a real witch and a stickler for rules and appearances?
- Do you feel like no one truly understands you anymore?

Folks, your life doesn't have to be as bleak and as boring as a gray day in Kansas. I'm Dorothy Gale, and I used to be just like you. My life was one series of misunderstandings, mishaps, and misguided beliefs—that is, until I found OZ—Dorothy Gale's OZ Complete Body and Soul Makeover System®.

Like a whirlwind through a Kansas trailer park, OZ changed my life. I'm happier. I'm healthier. I look younger, and I feel like a fairy princess! I'm over the rainbow with joy. And best of all, I'm more satisfied with my life, my relationships, and my home than ever before. Now I know there's no place like home, and with the OZ Complete Body and Soul Makeover Miracle, you can too!

If you've ever wondered what OZ can do for you, now's your chance. For a limited time, you can get my proven OZ Complete Body and Soul Makeover Miracle package, including:
- Easy-to-follow instructions to guide you on your journey through OZ.
- A series of soul-searching exercises to help you explore what you really want out of life.
- Repetitive affirmations to help you visualize your heart's desire.
- A pair of stylish, one-size-fits-most sparkly shoes to get you started on the right path. (They'll also reflect your new-found get-up-and-go attitude and show the world that you don't take no crap from the witches in this world who try to

interfere with your plans.)

When you've completed your journey through Dorothy Gale's OZ Complete Body and Soul Makeover Miracle package, you'll feel as if you've travelled over the rainbow and back without ever leaving your own backyard. You'll have a new outlook and a new attitude on life, love, and longevity. You'll feel like the streets are truly paved in gold and that the city is simply dripping in jewels – just for you! Your friends, your frenemies, and your family will marvel in amazement at the Brand New You.

You can't afford to pass up this incredible once-in-a-lifetime offer – it will change your life forever! If you order Dorothy Gale's OZ Complete Body and Soul Makeover Miracle package RIGHT NOW, you'll also receive my exclusive Emerald City Beauty Secrets bonus package. This limited edition offer will enable you to look thinner, feel better, and seem more youthful than ever. You can even dye your eyes to match your wardrobe!

But wait, there's more! Call now and you'll get my OZ Complete Body and Soul Makeover System, my exclusive Emerald City Beauty Secrets package, AND my limited edition Flying Monkey necklace, enhanced with genuine Swarovski Crystal embellishments on its life-like leather wings. You'll be the envy of all your friends!

You get all this for just three payments of $29.99 plus shipping and handling. It's a bargain at any price! I have such faith in the power of this offer to change your life that for today only, I'll double your order at no additional charge. You just pay the additional shipping and handling.

Don't delay. Call now!

Disclaimer: This offer is not available in stores. Dorothy Gale Inc. LLC does not take any responsibility for acid burns received while dissolving witches, injuries sustained during wind-driven transport, or unsightly stains caused by flying monkey poo. Side effects may include headache, listlessness, hallucinations, and/or bruising. If you or your little dog experience early onset menopause or erectile dysfunction while using any Dorothy Gale Inc. LLC product, that's a horse of a different color. No warranty or guarantee is offered or implied. You get what you pay for, my pretty! And your little dog, too.

About the Author

Allison Stein is an author, artist, TV addict, geek princess, and cat servant... not necessarily in that order. Her award-winning short fiction appears in "A Bubba In Time Saves None", "Houston, We've Got Bubbas" and "Flush Fiction" from Yard Dog Press. She also provided cover art for "Music For Four Hands", "Tick Hill" and "Diva", also from Yard Dog Press. When she's not painting, writing, tending her online shops, updating her social media status, or serving as cat furniture, she's a technical writer, software tester, and technology marketing communications specialist. (allisonstein.com, allisonstein.blogspot.com, @allisonstein on Twitter)

Oh, Them Silver Slippers

Laura J. Underwood

"Auntie Em, have you seen my slippers?" Dorothy asked.

"No, child, I haven't seen them," Auntie Emma replied.

"I would have sworn I had them here under the bed," Dorothy said.

She was wriggling around under the bed as Toto lie on the foot of it. The little dog watched her lacy-bottom britches moving around like some sort of wriggle worm, and then went back to chewing on the bit of leather that once used to hold the traces of the plow. Uncle Henry had cut it off and tossed it aside the other day, and Toto saw no reason to let a perfectly chewable piece of leather go to waste, especially since it was flavored with horse sweat and urine where it had been close enough to the horse's hind quarters and low enough that the beast could pee on it.

Dorothy came out from under the bed and looked at Toto. "Have you seen my slippers?" she asked and reached over to pet him. Instinctively, he growled and pulled the entire piece of leather into his mouth because she had taken such things away from him before. She didn't like it when he chewed on things.

What did she expect? He was a dog. Chewing was an integral part of his well being. Like rolling in horse manure and the road kills that occasionally could be found on the little dirt road that passed by their Kansas farm. Dogs had necessities, same as people. But for some reason, people thought dogs should not be allowed to do what came natural. Just because they didn't care for the stink...

Even now she squinted at him and frowned. "Toto, what have you got there? Is that one of my slippers? You bad dog, you. Give it here!"

She made a grab for the visible end of the trace, which in Toto's opinion, should have let her see it was not one of her slippers because they were on her feet right now, but then Dorothy had never been all that bright. Toto snapped and Dorothy squeaked in surprise and jerked her hand away, and that was the opening Toto needed to leap from the bed and scramble around the house.

She chased him through the house—a sight to see since it was only a single large room—demanding that he give back her slipper right now. He merely ran under the table, causing Auntie Emma to shriek, and then bolted for the screen door as Dorothy tried to dive under and grab him. One corner of it was torn where he had used it to get out before, and he streaked through that opening like a little rocket, charging across the porch and dropping into the dirt. Before she could get out of the house, he was under the porch, slipping through a small opening in the latticework. And there in the dark shade and cool earth, he settled down to continue chewing on the trace.

Dorothy exited the house, stumbled off the porch and stopped in the middle of the yard. She turned in circles, yelling, "Toto! Here, Toto! Please, Toto, where are you?"

He hated that whining simpering voice. Had hated it the whole time they were in Oz. She had used it every time she wanted to get something that no one wanted to give her.

Toto didn't care. He was in no mood to let her take anything away from him. Bad enough that Billina the hen was always stealing things from him without Dorothy doing the same.

Dorothy had tears running down her cheeks as she searched all around the house and even went looking around the hen house, but she couldn't find Toto. She plodded back into the house, her little heart broken.

This would never have happened if she had stayed in the Land of Oz. She missed the Scarecrow and the Tin Woodsman and even the Cowardly Lion. She had been someone of importance to them. And they had helped her with everything, from escaping the poppy field to getting to the home of Glinda, the good witch of the north.

Here, she was just Dorothy again. Granted, Auntie Em and Uncle Henry had been so much kinder to her when she survived the tornado that blew her off to Oz.

As she slipped back into the house, Auntie Emma was pounding dough to make bread. The old woman took one look at the young girl and shook her head.

"Child, what's got you all a' weeping now?" Auntie Em asked.

"Toto took one of my slippers," she said, and several more tears dribbled down her cheek, adding to the dramatic effect of it all.

"Are you sure of that?" Auntie Em asked. "Cos it looks to me like you're wearing your slippers."

"Oh," Dorothy said. She looked down and giggled. Yes, she was wearing her old worn-out leather slippers. "Oh, Auntie Em, I feel like such a little fool."

The look in Auntie Emma's eyes said that she agreed, but she shook her head and said, "Instead of accusing that poor dog of causing you trouble, you should learn to look. Now dry your eyes and don't worry about Toto. He'll be back when he's hungry."

Dorothy suddenly brightened up and smiled. "Of course, he will," she said more cheerfully, wiping her tears away. "Toto always comes back when he's hungry."

She glanced at the ratty old shoes on her feet and sighed.

"Now what?" Auntie Em asked.

"I just wish I hadn't lost those lovely silver slippers Glinda let me keep," she said. "They were so much prettier than these ratty old things."

"Those ratty old things keep your feet safe and warm unlike things you dream up, child," Auntie Em said. "Times are hard. You should be grateful that you have shoes. Now go on down to the barn and tell Uncle Henry that lunch will be ready in an hour. He frets if he don't think I'm making lunch."

Dorothy nodded and hopped off the stool and made for the door. Briefly, she stopped and wondered if it would be possible to fly with her own brown slippers. She even clicked her heels together and leaned forward a tad—and nearly fell flat on her face.

Auntie Em looked puzzled as Dorothy caught her balance and hurried out the door.

Toto watched as Dorothy walked off the porch and headed for the barn. He was tempted to follow her, but her attempt to steal his bit of trace was still fresh in his mind. So he waited until she had gone into the barn before he bolted out from under the porch. The piece of trace was history, shards in his stomach, and he was feeling the need to empty his bladder.

He marked the corner of the porch steps and scuffed the dirt with his hind feet, and then started to wander over towards the edge of the road.

On the far side was a vast plain of grey dust. They had come from that direction when they returned from that place smelling of funny little men and women and monkey butts. He admittedly had liked the smell of monkey butts, though he had not been too fond of the monkeys that owned them. They had grabbed him up and carried him through the air and teased him when he and Dorothy were prisoners of that witch woman that smelled like old rags and pissy men. Darned things were as bad as that stupid hen Billina.

Even now, he could see Billina pecking in the dust. Toto gave her wide berth as he hurried across the road to the desert's grey edge.

As Toto recalled, Dorothy had fallen when she took the last step, and he had been tossed off to one side. Stupid girl had lost those shiny shoes she was wearing. Toto had seen them fly off like a pair of sparkly butterflies when she hit the ground. One went east, and one went west, and they disappeared under the dust that coated everything. Toto had already found one of them just the other day, but just as he started to chew it, Billina the hen had pecked him and chased him away. Then she snatched it up and carried it into the hen house, and though Toto had wanted to follow and reclaim it, he knew better than to enter a house full of hens who would all come after him with their peckers.

Why the hen wanted the shoe, he didn't know. Stupid bird was probably hiding it in her nest, and that meant one day Dorothy might find it while looking for eggs.

The silver slipper had tasted good, what little he had managed to nibble of that silvery thing, and now he was of a mind to find the other one. If for no other reason than because he knew Dorothy would want to go back to Oz. It was all she talked about to him at night when she thought Uncle Henry and Auntie Em were fast asleep.

Toto had no desire to go there. He had hated the food. Hated the smell—well, except for the monkey butts.

He crossed the dusty road into the opposite field. Doggie ears twitching, he poked his nose into the grey dirt and started moving in first smaller then larger circles. And eventually, his nose uprooted the other silver slipper.

In the light of day, it practically glowed like a star. Toto picked it up in his terrier jaws and headed for the house.

But just as he started back across the road, Billina charged, clucking and flapping her wings. Damn the hen, she was trying to steal the last silver slipper.

She came at him like a speckled fury, wings beating him as she seized the silver slipper for a perch and rose over his head. Then she hit him with her pecker. Toto yelped and had to let go of the slipper.

It fell, Billina fell, and he darted back in to snatch it up before she could take it away.

Clucking furiously, the hen charged after him. Damn her, she was not going to give up. He ran full tilt under the porch, still carrying the slipper. Fortunately, Billini was too fat to get through the small hole. She stuck her head and most of her neck through, but because she kept flapping her wings, she could not follow.

Toto slid into the darkest corner he could find and started gnawing the slipper.

Dorothy heard the commotion at the house just as she and Uncle Henry were coming out of the barn. She saw Billina trying to get through that small hole in the lattice under the porch. Uncle Henry yelled at Billina because he didn't want the chickens laying eggs under the porch where no one could get to them. Dorothy watched her portly uncle suddenly move like a pumpkin down a hill, his gait bouncy and rolling and he waved his arms until Billina got the message. The hen squawked and fled for the chicken coop.

Uncle Henry stopped and gazed at the hole. Sweat rolled off him like a river, and he wheezed until Dorothy feared he would pop. But then Auntie Em called out, "Lunch is ready." He tore off looking at the hole and grumbled under his breath about stupid hens.

"Remind me to fix that after lunch," he said.

Dorothy giggled and followed him into the house.

Toto finished chewing the silvery shoe, swallowing the shards. They had a strange unnatural sweetness to them. Dogs preferred things that tasted like meat or dead things. The shoes were not at all what he would have imagined in his doggy brain. Still he chewed it up good, and swallowed every bite before sneaking towards the hole in the lattice.

Billina was strutting around the yard with the other hens. Maybe Toto could get to the hen house and fetch that other slipper now. He squeezed through his small opening, staying close to the foundations and working his way around the house, ever wary of the irritable hen and her adoring flock.

The hen house stood before him, a little ramshackle and covered with depression dust like everything else on the farm. It stank of hen poop and chicken feed. Toto glanced back over his shoulder. He could not see the hens. He slunk up the ramp and slipped into the smelly dark.

Temptation was to start rolling in the poop, but of course, that would take time, and he didn't know how much he had. Being a dog, he really had no need for measuring the passing of time. Still, it would not be good to be caught in the hen house at all, so he hurried over to the biggest nest, sniffing as he went. Then he crawled up into the nest and started to dig through the packed down straw, and was rewarded with two eggs and the silver slipper.

The eggs were tempting, but he left them alone, grabbed the shoe and darted for the opening of the hen house...

...And slid to a halt because there was Billina and the rest of the hens rounding the corner. She took one look at him standing there in the opening with the slipper in his mouth and gave a loud squawk. And like an army, the rest of the hens followed her, charging across the yard to the coop.

Toto decided it was time to leave, and leaping from the ramp, he ran for the barn. Fortunately, he had a good head start, but the hens were determined to catch him, especially Billina. He bolted through the doors of the barn and made it into the first stall just as the hens came charging through the opening. Refusing to let go of the slipper, Toto crawled under a horse trough.

He could hear the hens clucking and strutting around. Then the sound of Henry shouting in rage because all the hens were in the barn, and he never wanted them there because it took too long to find the eggs. They all ran, all save Billina who looked into the stall where Toto hid. She was giving him that, "I'll get you, little dog," look that he hated to admit scared the willies out of him, and for a moment, he feared she was going to charge.

But then Uncle Henry shouted, and Billina had to run with the rest of her flock.

Relieved, Toto settled into chewing the other silver slipper to shreds.

Later in the day, Dorothy saw Toto coming out of the barn. He was moving slowly as though something bothered him.

"There you are, you naughty little Toto," Dorothy said. She noticed he seemed to cringe as she crossed the yard at a silly mad dash that kicked up the dust. But he didn't flee as she reached down and snatched him up in her arms.

He just went "ARRRRRRRPPPPP!" so loud in her ear, and his

hot doggy breath had a strange sweet smell.

"What have you been eating Toto?" Dorothy said and promptly held him out at arm's length to look at him. He didn't look so well. "Poor, poor Toto, I bet you're starving for a good meal."

His little ears went flat, and his tail didn't wag at all. But she loved him so much, and she drew him close and ran all the way to the house, bouncing him roughly.

Maybe he just needed something good to eat to perk him up.

The jog was not doing Toto's stomach any good. For all his excitement at getting to eat the second silver slipper in peace, he felt it rumbling in his stomach like a bad vibration. Getting shaken like a martini mixer was not helping.

Dorothy, however, did not seem to notice his discomfort. She charged the entire distance to the house, bounding him around until she popped through the screen door screeching, "Auntie Em, I think Toto is hungry now."

Auntie Em was looking a little puzzled as Dorothy sat Toto on the floor. He wobbled a couple of time, his little guts rendering some terrible sounds.

"See, his poor tummy is rumbling from hunger," Dorothy said. "What shall we give him?"

Auntie Em frowned. "Well, I suppose he can have the leftovers," she said, looking at the pitiful remains of their last meal.

Food? Toto perked up just a bit. He was a dog. Gorging was part of his nature. Auntie Emma was dumping delicious smelling things into his bowl and filling another with water and sitting them on the floor. He charged over and began to wolf down the lunch until his belly felt like it was going to burst.

Which of course, it did in a way. Dogs are curiously gluttonous, but they don't always hold down what they eat. He felt the rumbling so powerful that there was nothing he could do to stop the sudden rush that emerged from his mouth. Food, silver slippers and all, it rushed out of him in a wave. Auntie Em gasped and then choked. Dorothy screamed.

"Lord have mercy, what has that dog been eating?" Auntie Em asked as she covered her nose.

"Oh, look, Toto barfed something sparkly!" Dorothy said.

Toto made a dive to reclaim it, but Dorothy suddenly pushed him aside.

"My silver slippers!" she cried. "Toto, you naughty dog you! You ate my silver slippers. How am I ever going to get back to Oz?"

Toto looked at the sparkly mess, turned on his heels and headed for the door.

He suddenly wondered if he could take a roll in the chicken coop before Billina and the other hens pecked him to death.

It had to smell better than monkey butt.

Then again...

About the Author

Laura J. Underwood has never been to Oz, but she read *The Wonderful Wizard of Oz* as a child and always wanted a flying monkey for a pet. Her parents never obliged her, so she took to writing about flying horses and fantasy creatures instead. She is the author of *Ard Magister*, *Dragon's Tongue*, *Wandering Lark* and a host of other novels, novellas and short stories too numerous to put in this bio (because it would be as long as her story if not longer). She sold her first efforts to Marion Zimmer Bradley in 1987, and to date has over two hundred published items to her credit. Laura lives in East Tennessee, where they often see a lot of tornados passing through. Fortunately, she does not live in the trailer parks that always get hit by them. When not writing, she is a librarian who likes to play with beads, draw, play a little harp and watch bad movies. She is an active member of SFWA, and her webpage is located at http://www.sff.net/people/keltora

Dorothy Down Under

Glenn R. Sixbury

"Tell me again."

"I've already told you a hundred times," Dorothy said. "I made the story up. I made it all up."

White haired and stern, Dr. Porter leaned forward and peered through his wire-rimmed glasses at a notebook that lay open on his huge oak desk. "Your Aunt Emily stated otherwise. She says you were like a dog worrying over a bone. Both she and your Uncle Henry told you it was just a bad dream, but you refused to believe them. They think that's why you became violent."

"I didn't become violent. I threw a rock through the front window."

Dr. Porter raised his eyebrows.

"I didn't hurt anyone!"

"Yet now you claim you made the story up?" He checked his notes again. "After two weeks of extra chores at home, you refused to change your story. Even after a week in this facility, you continued to claim what you experienced was real. Now, just a few days later, it's a mere fabrication. Why the sudden reversal?"

The ceiling fan creaked as it spun overhead. Dorothy glanced at the medical certificates on the wall, careful to look anywhere but straight ahead.

Dr. Porter didn't wait for an answer. "Claiming you invented your story won't allow you to go home. Instead we must attack the root of your delusion. I believe I've found a way to do that."

Dorothy wasn't sure she would ever go home. After she threw the rock through the window, Auntie Em said that Dorothy had dropped her basket and that she needed special doctors to help her pick it up again. That's when they loaded up the pickup and brought her to the sanatorium near Norton.

Dr. Porter opened a desk drawer, pulled out a familiar pair of shoes, and set them on his huge blotter.

Dorothy gasped. The shoes from Oz. "Where'd you get those? They were lost."

He smiled. "So you admit these are *the* shoes? The *magic* shoes? The ones you told your aunt and uncle about?"

She nodded.

"Put them on."

She hesitated. This had to be a trick.

"It's important for your therapy, Dorothy. You want to get better, don't you?"

She pulled off her hospital slippers and jammed the shoes onto her feet. After jumping out of the chair, she rapidly clicked her heels together three times. "There's no place like home! There's no place like home! There's no place like home!"

She waited for the sudden lurch, the spinning, the queasy whirl in the pit of her stomach that would tell her she'd traveled back to the farm. But nothing happened. Slowly she opened her eyes.

Dr. Porter beamed like a kid on Christmas morning. "Now we're making progress!"

Grabbing the paperweight from his desk, she threw it at him.

Rosy snorted. "You mean you hit the ol' coot with his own paperweight? I'da loved to see that!"

"I shouldn't have done it," Dorothy said.

"Nonsense, Dottie. He had it comin'. All men need to be hit once in a while."

Still shy of thirty according to her, Rosy was pretty but she always wore too much makeup. A lit cigarette, its butt end stained lipstick red, jutted from a corner of Rosy's mouth. The cigarette bobbed whenever Rosy talked. Dorothy always expected it to fall out, but it never did.

"What I wouldn't do for a drink."

"They have a water fountain in the hallway."

Rosy rolled her eyes. "Not that kind of drink, kid."

"Oh," Dorothy said, confused. Then her eyes widened. "Oh!"

Dorothy and Rosy were sitting around a folding table in the community room. A jigsaw puzzle with half the pieces missing lay abandoned on the table like the bottom off a rusted-through sauce pan. Various other patients, the ward's less dangerous ones, were sitting or standing around the room in small groups. Most were smoking as they talked. A few stared out the open windows at the empty prairie longing for a breeze that wouldn't blow. One old woman sat in the corner, drooling.

"Don't go all high and mighty on me," Rosy said. "Out here in Carrie Nation country, y'all might drink a lot of iced tea, but back at the club, a drink's a drink's a drink, ya know?"

Rosy popped her bubble gum, as if to emphasize the point.

Dorothy had already heard all about the club. A jazz club on Kansas City's south side, Rosy had worked there since she was fifteen. There and around, Rosy had said. Dorothy wasn't sure what "around" meant, but it couldn't be anything good.

"What's it like to work as a cigarette girl?" Dorothy asked.

Rosy laughed. "Why? You lookin' for a job?"

"Why, no ma'am," Dorothy said. "I didn't mean that."

"Course you didn't," Rosy took out her compact case and dabbed powder on her nose. "It's nothin' you'd need to think about. There ain't no choice for women like me. It weren't my fault I had to drop out of school after barely startin' the sixth grade. My old man was ailin' from all the whiskey he poured down his throat. Weren't his fault, neither. Just the way things are. Like us being here, ya know? I'd like to change it, but I ain't never been bright enough for anything else."

Peering into the compact's small mirror, Rosy applied more lipstick. "Oh, and darlin'. I prefer candy girl to cigarette girl. Cigarettes are dirty and candy's sweet."

"They're both dirty if you ask me." A tall, thin woman carrying a ragged book stepped briskly around their table and sat down.

Rosy snapped her compact closed and put the lipstick away. Then she pried open her distinctive Red Lion cigarette case. "Don't be sayin' that, Josie. I ain't as smart as you but I can call myself what I want."

"My name isn't Josie. It's Joscelin."

Rosy lit a fresh cigarette. "That's exactly right, Josie. I'll try to remember that."

Josie opened her book and quoted from it like a Baptist preacher:

> THERE was a road ran past our house
> Too lovely to explore
> I asked my mother once—she said
> That if you followed where it led
> It brought you to the milk-man's door.
> (That's why I have not traveled more.)

Josie slammed the book shut. "I've told you before, Rosy. When you work in that club, you become nothing more than a slave, serving the baser instincts of man by degrading yourself and your body."

"Ya, but the tips are good."

Josie grunted.

Dorothy liked to listen to Josie talk. She always used such big words and seemed so sure about everything she said. A dignified looking woman, probably around forty, Josie hadn't spoken to Dorothy until a couple days ago. She said she didn't like short-timers, but that after a week, it looked like Dorothy might be around for a while and so it was about time they got to know each other.

Alice slid into the last seat at their four-person table. As always, she had her stuffed bear, Mr. Goodwin, clutched in one arm. A short, plump girl only a few years older than Dorothy, Alice wore no makeup at all. Her hair was uncombed and she reeked like a hog pen on a hot day, but she'd been nice to Dorothy all along.

"It's not proper to talk about men and bodies," Alice whispered. "I heard you and it's not right. Not right at all."

"So says you." Josie laughed. "You wouldn't be making that claim if those men were adorned in yellow."

Alice hugged Mr. Goodwin tightly and began squirming in her chair, as if she had to go to the bathroom and was having problems holding it.

Josie grinned. "Giant yellow pajamas, just like the ones Nero Wolfe always wears. Yards and yards of silky yellow—"

"Stop it," Alice hissed and squirmed even more. She was squeezing Mr. Goodwin so tightly the stitches were about to pop. "Stop it, stop it, stop it!"

"Cut it out!" Rosy flicked her lit cigarette at Josie's face.

The butt bounced off Josie's cheek and the cigarette landed in her lap. Josie leaped from the chair and danced around, swatting at her cotton dress.

Alice giggled, and Dorothy couldn't help grinning.

"I ought to. . . ." Josie started.

"Ought to what?" Rosy stood and stared up at Josie. Rosy was a full six inches shorter and maybe twenty pounds lighter than Josie, but nobody wanted to cross her when she was on the scrap.

Josie hesitated, then silently took her seat.

The tension disappeared from Rosy's shoulders and her face relaxed into her normal easy expression. "Don't be so mean all the time, Josie. Alice can't help it, no more than I can. And it ain't your fault your father used to beat you—"

"I told you that in strictest confidence!"

"And I was confident when I said it."

"Midget!" Josie said it like a cuss word. Rosy stiffened.

Dorothy had heard part of the story. It's why Rosy was here. Three midgets in loud suits had been a bit fresh with her at work, and she'd beaten them all within an inch of their lives. Rosy didn't like midgets.

"Just think about it," Josie went on. "Fat little fingers, pulling at you, touching you. Greasy little sausages on your knee, moving up toward your thigh. Dozens of little men in brightly colored clothes, all coming for you."

Rosy slapped the ashtray in Josie's direction. Josie yelped as it landed in her lap, and a cloud of gray ash exploded around her like a dust storm rolling in from the south. Rosy darted around the table, her fists raised, her nose stopping only inches from Josie's face.

"Stop it!" Dorothy shouted. "Stop it, both of you!"

"What's goin' on now, ladies?" The tall orderly shuffled over to their table, cracking his knuckles as he approached.

All four women froze. For a moment, none of them even breathed.

"Nothing," Rosy said. "Just knocked over the ashtray is all."

Rosy immediately stepped away from Josie, then bent over and started scraping the lipstick-stained butts back into the ashtray.

The orderly squared himself in front of Rosy, grabbed her hair, and pulled her head back until she was looking straight up at him. "Any more trouble and I'll have to take you back to your room. Understand me, Rosy?"

Rosy's gaze flicked down toward the powerful man's waist, then back up again. The wild look in her eyes reminded Dorothy of a frightened colt. Rosy nodded as best she could and the orderly released his hold on her hair.

When he was out of earshot, Josie said, "Why doesn't he just visit the TB ward? I'm sure he'd garner plenty of volunteers there who'd be willing to service him."

Rosy spoke in a harsh whisper. "I don't want him serviced. I want him dead. If I could, I'd kill him myself."

Alice let out a terrified squeak and rocked back and forth, clinging to Mr. Goodwin. "Don't say that. Oh, don't say that. You say that and bad things happen. Night comes, and then it's bad. Always bad. No yellow. Even the moon turns black."

"It don't matter," Rosy said. "Nobody can't do nothing to harm me. I'm only good for one thing. Ain't bright enough for anything else."

"That's not true. My Auntie Em always says that you can do anything you put your mind to."

Rosy brightened a bit, but Josie barked a single laugh. "Is that the same aunt who sent you here?"

Dorothy didn't answer and they all fell silent.

"Don't be givin' Dottie no grief." Rosie grinned. "It ain't her fault neither. She's crazy as a shithouse rat. Aren't you, Dottie?"

"Well, I never," Dorothy said.

Rosy winked at her. "I'm sure you will someday, if we ever get outta here."

Josie arched one eyebrow.

Alice whispered, "Dirty, dirty, dirty."

"I'm just joshin' you," Rosy said. "It ain't like we don't all have problems. That's why we're all cooped up here together out in the middle of nowhere. So we don't *hurt* no one."

Rosy laughed at her own comment, but Josie straightened and said, "I've never hurt anyone."

"What about the monkeys?"

"They don't count. They're disgusting animals. None of them deserve to live. They throw filth at each other. They threw it at me."

"And so you shot them?" Rosy laughed again.

"Not immediately," Josie said defensively. "I had to go home first. To retrieve my husband's shotgun."

Rosy whispered to Dorothy. "The monkeys were in the zoo."

Josie's eyes focused on something far away. "Such a glorious sight. Monkey parts flying everywhere. But some of the foul things lived. People stopped me before I could finish. They took it way. The gun. I tried to finish, but they wouldn't let me. The men. It's always men."

"At least you have one," Rosy said. "Poor old Alice here ... all she wants is a tall, handsome man in a yellow suit. As if any man would ever wear a yellow suit."

"He might." Alice tilted her head, a pleasant grin spreading across her face.

"If he did," Josie said glumly, "he'd probably have a pet monkey."

They all laughed until the orderly glared and cracked his knuckles again.

"Say, Dottie. You never did explain what Dr. Sourpuss did to make you mad enough to bean him with his own paper weight. Did he touch you in places he's not allowed?"

Dorothy's face grew hot. "No. Nothing like that. He just gave me back my shoes."

Josie's eyes widened. "You hit him because he gave you a pair of shoes?"

Rosy cupped one hand to the side of her mouth. She leaned toward Josie conspiratorially, but spoke in a normal voice. "Told ya. Crazy as a shit house rat."

Dorothy pulled at the stiff collar of her dress. "It's not just the shoes. He laughed at me, too."

"Did he now?" Rosy whistled. "Imagine that. I didn't even know he could laugh."

"I guess he didn't exactly laugh. He was just—well—he was just so happy!"

"Damn straight. I'da hit him, too. What gives him the right to be so damned happy when we're all miserable?"

"You don't understand. I'm not miserable. Not very much, anyway. I just don't want to stay here anymore. The doctor can't help me. No one can."

Rosy patted her arm. "There's no one that can help any of us, darlin'. I'm dumb as a post, Josie has the charm of a rabid wolverine, and Alice wets herself every time a man wearing a yellow bow tie walks into the room."

Josie harrumphed. Alice giggled. Dorothy shook her head violently. "You're not dumb, Rosy. You just haven't finished your schooling is all."

"I haven't finished a lot of things," Rosy admitted.

"Hold it," Dorothy said. "That's it. Why didn't I see it before?"

"See what?" Rosy asked.

"In Oz! Glinda said the shoes had the power, but I don't think that's true. Don't you see? I helped the scarecrow, and the tin woodman, and the lion. I thought the wizard helped them, but it wasn't the wizard at all. It was me! Why'd it take me so long to understand? It's no wonder the shoes didn't work in Dr. Porter's office. They didn't have any power. I'd already used it up getting home."

"What are you babbling about, girl?" Josie asked.

Rosy pointed at Dorothy, twirled a finger around her temple, and then winked.

"I'm not crazy," Dorothy said. "I'm really not, and I can prove it to you."

Rosy violently flicked her ashes into the small tin ashtray. "Uh-huh. All I'm saying is you better not call up a flock of flying monkeys with those weird shoes of yours because I don't think Josie could take it."

"Flying monkeys?" Josie started to her feet, her eyes wide.

Rosy nodded. "I'll explain it to you later, after you've had your meds."

Dorothy wrinkled her brow until it hurt. "Don't distract me. Doin' magic isn't easy."

Josie settled back into her seat. She twisted the old book in her hands and glanced at the orderly. Dorothy hoped she wouldn't call out to him. She didn't want to be interrupted. She almost understood it all. Helping others produced the power to help herself.

Suddenly Dorothy smiled. "I've got it. Give me your compact, Rosy."

"Why? You gettin' ready to go somewhere?"

Dorothy ignored her. "Alice, please hand me Mr. Goodwin."

Alice hesitated. She clutched Mr. Goodwin with both arms and her gaze flitted left and right between Rosy and Josie. Only when Rosy nodded and smiled at her did she hand the shabby bear over. At the same time, Rosy surrendered her compact.

Dorothy turned to Josie. "And your book. May I see it, please?"

Josie clutched her well-read copy of *A Few Figs from Thistles*. "No! You don't need it."

"*I* don't need it," Dorothy said, "but there's someone at this table who does."

Josie clutched the book and shook her head. Rosie prompted, "It's alright, Josie. I think I see where she's goin' with this."

Dorothy was staring at Josie, but noticed motion out of the corner of her eye. She turned her head and caught Rosy with her arms hugging her own shoulders as if they'd been pulled there by the sleeves of a straightjacket.

"I know what it sounds like, but you need to trust me. I know what I'm doing." Dorothy's voice shook as she said the words. She took several deep breaths, trying to remain calm, and tried again. "Please, Josie. This is your chance to help someone."

Josie surrendered the book.

Dorothy smiled. "Good. Now, don't rush me. I doubt I'll do this as well as the wizard, but here goes."

She thrust Josie's book at Rosy. "You didn't get the chance to finish your education, but people don't have to go to school to be smart. They just are or they aren't, and I can tell that you are. But not everybody can see that as well as me. So I have a solution. Memorize all the poems in this book. Whenever you're not feeling as smart as the people around you, quote the poem that's in keeping with the current situation. That way, you'll sound smart, and it'll help people to see you for who you really are."

Rosy looked at the book, then up at Dorothy, then back at the book again. Her brow wrinkled and she cocked her head, but after a loud pop of her gum, she reached out and took the book.

Dorothy smiled broadly. "Good. And Alice. Sweet Alice. You'd like to meet that man in the yellow suit, wouldn't you?"

Alice nodded vigorously.

Dorothy presented her with Rosy's compact. "Beauty is in the eye of the beholder. But what they see isn't just about what's there. It also comes from the confidence of the person being looked at. If you feel pretty, you will be pretty. But you'll need to help that feeling along. Take a bath at least once a week, brush your hair twice a day, and whenever you're not feeling pretty, put on some of Rosy's powder and you'll be as pretty as any lady ever could be. Can you do that for me?"

Alice looked confused but she took the compact. After turning it over several times in her hands, she lifted her gaze to Dorothy and smiled her shy smile.

Dorothy turned toward Josie.

"You're the toughest one of all, Josie, because you're like a watermelon that's been kept too long."

"I'm what?"

"You're hard on the outside, but I can see that you're really soft on the inside. That hard shell is what's keeping you from being happy."

"It's the filthy, stinking monkeys that are keeping me from being happy. And what's this about flying monkeys? What kind of horror is that? Who's ever heard of such a thing?"

"Please, Josie. Just take this."

Dorothy held out Mr. Goodwin.

"The bear?"

"It's not a monkey." Dorothy smiled. "It's soft. It's defenseless. It's something for you to watch over. Take care of Mr. Goodwin. Learn to love him and you'll be able to love anyone. Even the people who put you here."

Josie folded her arms. "I'm not taking that old bear. It's filthy and it *smells!*"

"Take it," Dorothy urged.

Rosy grinned. "If I can force myself to read this god-awful book, you can give a little lovin' to that ol' bear."

Josie shook her head.

Alice's voice quavered as she said, "It's Mr. Goodwin. Don't you like Mr. Goodwin?"

Josie's eyes flicked in Alice's direction. Slowly, her arms unfolded. With a sudden swipe, she snatched the bear out of Dorothy's hand. "There! You happy now?"

Dorothy smiled. "Yes. Now I can go."

"Go?" Josie asked in a gruff voice. "You can't go anywhere. If you carry on like this, Dr. Porter will never let you out of here."

Dorothy took a long last look around the table. "Don't worry. I'll send you all a postcard."

Without getting up, she closed her eyes. She couldn't return home. That place was lost to her forever. Instead she would go as far away from Kansas as possible. They'd need to speak English there, because she didn't know any other languages. That made the choice easy. Concentrating hard, she said, "There's no place like Australia."

"Huh? Dottie, what are you—hey, stop that!" Rosy sounded worried. "What's wrong with her eyes? What's she staring at?"

As soon as Dorothy's heels touched, the first wave of magic bubbled up and blurred her vision. She repeated her phrase and clicked her heels together again, releasing more of the magic. "There's no place like Australia."

"Quit it, Dorothy. This isn't funny!" It was Josie. Her voice shook, and her hands grabbed the sides of Dorothy's face. The next words she spoke came from a long way off. "I can't keep her head from shaking. Quick! Rosy! Get the orderly!"

The world twisted. Dorothy felt a giant hand reach through her body and grab her navel, ready to jerk her away from this terrible place. Bells rang and bees buzzed. Dorothy smelled burning flesh, like when Auntie Em singed the skin of a plucked chicken. The magic, liquid fire, burned through every part of her. Its pain felt good. Just once more.

Dorothy brought her heels apart. As she started them together, she readied herself to speak the final words, the ones that would set her free. So close now. So very close. Warm wind whipped across her face and ruffled her hair. Tiny lights sparkled behind her closed eyes.

Alice's scream was followed by a litany of "No! No! No! No! No! No! No!"

"There's no place like Australia!"

Dorothy's heels touched and the feeling of falling consumed her. The cold tile of the floor struck her hard on the face. Then the world twisted, and she spun uncontrollably. Awful blackness swallowed her and nausea slammed against her in waves. Her fingernails dug painfully into her palms.

One step. Two steps. Three.

She pulled her new world into existence around her. Slowly she opened her eyes. The sunshine was too bright, too hot. With a thought, it dimmed. Beneath her fingers, she felt dry grass. Warm wind played with her hair. Birds chirped. She smelled fresh air and inhaled deeply, relishing this new and wonderful world.

But had the shoes taken her where she'd asked? She sat alone beneath a clear blue sky, the hot summer sun overhead. Scrub trees and clumps of yellow grass surrounded her for as far as she could see. Was this Kansas? No. The dirt was too red. Perhaps Oklahoma.

Dorothy stood up. She immediately spotted several buttes in the distance. Definitely not Kansas. And then she saw the kangaroos bouncing over the scrub brush, their reddish brown coats catching the sun, their long tails bobbing with each hop.

She smiled. She'd made it. Free.

Suddenly hooves sounded behind her, quickly growing closer. She spun around to see what was coming and readied herself to run. What kind of dangerous wild creatures did they have in Australia?

A man on horseback thundered up and yanked his mount to a stop. "What kinda drongo's gone walkabout 'cross my land—holy dooley! You're a Sheila! What? Are you ga-ga then?"

Dorothy blinked at him. She'd been told they spoke English in Australia. Now she wasn't so sure. She curtsied. "Very pleased to meet you sir. I'm from Kansas."

"Kansas? What? From the US?"

"I'm from the United States, if that's what you mean. My name is Dorothy."

The stranger was covered in dust. Beads of sweat dotted his face and the underarms of his long-sleeved shirt were soaked. She'd always thought the people in Australia would be nice. Now she wasn't so sure.

A squat bluish gray dog ran up beside the horse. Dorothy took a step back, but the man gave a short whistle. The dog sat down and cocked his head, staring intently. With a start she realized each eye was a different color.

With a flourish the man took off his hat and inclined his head forward. "Beg your pardon, ma'am. I didn't mean to be a bogan. My name's Jack. It's just that we're way beyond the black stump out here. It's a day's ride to the nearest village. Heck, it'd take you a couple hours just to walk off my ranch."

Dorothy glanced around. His ranch. A couple hours walk. This was certainly looking better than the sanatorium. She gave Jack her best smile and curtsied again. "I'd be happy to explain all about my situation, but it's a rather long story. I don't suppose you'd have a bit of shade and a cool drink of water."

Jack smiled. His teeth caught the sun in a perfect flash of white. "Course I do. Come along. We'll see what we can do."

Jack reached a hand toward her. She took it, and with a stomach-lurching pull, he lifted her up behind him. She settled on the rear of the horse. "Hold tight, now."

She put her arms around him and felt the hard muscles in his belly tense beneath her fingers. As the horse started forward, she said, "That town you mentioned. Does it have a place where I could buy a postcard? I've got some friends trapped in Kansas who are waiting to hear from me."

About the Author

Glenn R. Sixbury is the author of the novel, *Legacy*. You can find his stories in several Marion Zimmer Bradley anthologies and several of Yard Dog's other anthologies. Glenn teaches classes on writing and has led sessions for writing workshops at worldcons and local writing conventions. He's currently working on a non-fiction book on writing called *The Wonderful Writing Secrets of Oz*.

The link to Oz comes naturally for Glenn, since he's spent most of his life on the dusty prairies of Kansas. Currently he lives just a poppy field away from Wamego, Kansas, which is home to the Oz Museum, the Oz Winery, Toto's Tacoz, an annual festival known as OZtoberFEST, a Yellow Brick Road bike ride, the Poppyfield art gallery, and Uncle Henry's Antiques. Wamego's even building a genuine yellow brick road.

About the Cover Artist

Brad W Foster is an illustrator, cartoonist, writer, publisher, and whatever other labels he can use to get through the door! He's won the Fan Artist Hugo a few times, picked up a Chesley award, and turned a bit of self-publishing started about thirty years ago into the Jabberwocky Graphix publishing empire. (Total number of "employees": himself and his wife Cindy.) His strange drawings and cartoons have appeared in over a thousand science fiction fanzines. On a more professional level he has worked as an illustrator for various genre magazines, the better known among those being *Amazing Stories* and *Dragon*. In comics he had his own series some years back, "The Mechthings," and even got to play with the big boys for a few years as the official "Big Background Artist" of Image Comic's "Shadowhawk."

Outside our beloved genre it is possible you've seen more of his work in titles as varied as "Cat Fancy", "Cavalier," or "Highlights for Children." Most recently he has done covers for Yard Dog and Zumaya books, illustrations for magazines such as "Space & Time," "Talebones" and "Leading Edge," and has even managed to work a dragon into the official poster for the Oktoberfest in Tulsa, Oklahoma!

Yard Dog Press Titles As Of This Print Date

A Bubba In Time Saves None
Edited by Selina Rosen

A Glimpse of Splendor and Other Stories
Dave Creek

A Man, A Plan, (yet lacking) A Canal, Panama
Linda Donahue

Adventures of the Irish Ninja
Selina Rosen

All the Marbles
Dusty Rainbolt

Almost Human
Gary Moreau

Ard Magister
Laura J. Underwood

Black Rage
Selina Rosen

Blackrose Avenue
Mark Shepherd

The Boat Man
Selina Rosen

Bobby's Troll
John Lance

Bogie Woods
Laura J. Underwood

Bride of Tranquility
Tracy S. Morris

Bruce and Roxanne Save the World... Again!
Rie Sheridan

The Bubba Chronicles
Selina Rosen

Bubbas Of the Apocalypse
Edited by Selina Rosen

Chains of Redemption
Selina Rosen

Checking On Culture
Lee Killough

Chronicles of the Last War
Laura J. Underwood

Dadgum Martians Invade the Lucky Nickel Saloon
Ken Rand

Dark & Stormy Nights
Bradley H. Sinor

Deja Doo
Edited by Selina Rosen

Diva
Mark W. Tiedemann

Dracula's Lawyer
Julia S. Mandala

The Essence of Stone
Beverly A. Hale

Extensions
Mark Tiedemann

Fairy BrewHaHa at the Lucky Nickel Saloon
Ken Rand

Fire & Ice
Selina Rosen

Flush Fiction, Volume I: Stories To Be Read In One Sitting
Edited by Selina Rosen

The Four Bubbas of the Apocalypse: Flatulence, Halitosis, Incest, and... Ned
Edited by Selina Rosen

The Four Redheads: Apocalypse Now!
Linda L. Donahue, Rhonda Eudaly, Julia S. Mandala, & Dusty Rainbolt

The Four Redheads of the Apocalypse
Linda L. Donahue, Rhonda Eudaly,
Julia S. Mandala, & Dusty Rainbolt

The Garden In Bloom
Jeffrey Turner

The Golems Of Laramie County
Ken Rand

The Guardians
Lynn Abbey

Hammer Town
Selina Rosen

The Happiness Box
Beverly A. Hale

The Host Series:
The Host
Fright Eater
Gang Approval
Selina Rosen

Houston, We've Got Bubbas!
Edited by Selina Rosen

I Should Have Stayed In Oz
Edited by Selina Rosen

Illusions of Sanity
James K. Burk

In the Shadows
Bradley H. Sinor

International House of Bubbas
Edited by Selina Rosen

The Killswitch Review
Steven-Elliot Altman
Diane DeKelb-Rittenhouse

It's the Great Bumpkin,
Cletus Brown!
Katherine A. Turski

The Leopard's Daughter
Lee Killough

The Long, Cold Walk To Mars
Jeffrey Turner

Marking the Signs and Other
Tales Of Mischief
Laura J. Underwood

Material Things
Selina Rosen

Medieval Misfits
Tracy S. Morris

Mirror Images
Susan Satterfield

Music for Four Hands
Lou Antonelli & Edward Morris

More Stories That Won't Make Your
Parents Hurl
Edited by Selina Rosen

My Life with Geeks and Freaks
Claudia Christian

The Necronomicrap:
A Guide To Your Horooscope
Tim Frayser

Pathfinder I
Wm. Mark Simmons

Playing With Secrets
Bradley H & Sue P. Sinor

Prophecy of Swords
M.H. Bonham

Reruns
Selina Rosen

Rock 'n' Roll Universe
Ken Rand

The Runestone of Teiwas
M.H. Bonham

Serpent Singer and Other Stories
M.H. Bonham

Shadow Lord
Laura J. Underwood

Shadows In Green
Richard Dansky

Stories That Won't Make Your Parents Hurl
Edited by Selina Rosen

Strange Twists Of Fate
James K. Burk

Tales From the Home for Wayward Spirits and Bar-B-Que Grill
Rie Sheridan

Tales Of the Lucky Nickel Saloon, Second Ave., Laramie, Wyoming, U S of A
Ken Rand

Texistani: Indo-Pak Food From A Texas Kitchen
Beverly A. Hale

That's All Folks
J. F. Gonzalez

Through Wyoming Eyes
Ken Rand

Turn Left to Tomorrow
Robin Wayne Bailey

Wings of Morning
Katharine Eliska Kimbriel

Zombies In Oz and Other Undead Musings
Robin Wayne Bailey

Double Dog (A YDP Imprint):

1:
Of Stars & Shadows
Mark W. Tiedemann
This Instance Of Me
Jeffrey Turner

#2:
Gods and Other Children
Bill D. Allen
Tranquility
Tracy Morris

#3:
Home Is the Hunter
James K. Burk
Farstep Station
Lazette Gifford

#4:
Sabre Dance
Melanie Fletcher
The Lunari Mask
Laura J. Underwood

#5:
House of Doors
Julia Mandala
Jaguar Moon
Linda A. Donahue

Just Cause (A YDP Imprint):

Black Rage
Selina Rosen

How I Survived the Apocolypse
Selina Rosen

Non-YDP titles we distribute:

Chains of Freedom
Chains of Destruction
Jabone's Sword
Queen of Denial
Recycled
Strange Robby
Sword Masters
Selina Rosen

Three Ways to Order:

1. Write us a letter telling us what you want, then send it along with your check or money order (made payable to Yard Dog Press) to: Yard Dog Press, 710 W. Redbud Lane, Alma, AR 72921-7247

2. Use selinarosen@cox.net or lynnstran@cox.net to contact us and place your order. Then send your check or money order to the address above. *This has the advantage of allowing you to check on the availability of short-stock items such as T-shirts and back-issues of Yard Dog Comics.*

3. Contact us as in #1 or #2 above and pay with a credit card or by debit from your checking account. Either give us the credit card information in your letter/Email/phone call, or go to our website and use our shopping carts. If you send us your information, please include your name as it appears on the card, your credit card number, the expiration date, and the 3 or 4-digit security code after your signature on the back (CVV). Please remember that we will include media rate (minimum $3.00) S/H for mailing in the lower 48 states.

Watch our website at
www.yarddogpress.com
for news of upcoming projects
and new titles!!

A Note to Our Readers

We at Yard Dog Press understand that many people buy used books because they simply can't afford new ones. That said, and understanding that not everyone is made of money, we'd like you to know something that you may not have realized. Writers only make money on new books that sell. At the big houses a writer's entire future can hinge on the number of books they sell. While this isn't the case at Yard Dog Press, the honest truth is that when you sell or trade your book or let many people read it, the writer and the publishing house aren't making any money.

As much as we'd all like to believe that we can exist on love and sweet potato pie, the truth is we all need money to buy the things essential to our daily lives. Writers and publishers are no different.

We realize that these "freebies" and cheap books often turn people on to new writers and books that they wouldn't otherwise read. However we hope that you will reconsider selling your copy, and that if you trade it or let your friends borrow it, you also pass on the information that if they really like the author's work they should consider buying one of their books at full price sometime so that the writer can afford to continue to write work that entertains you.

We appreciate all our readers and *depend* upon their support.

Thanks,
The Editorial Staff
Yard Dog Press

PS – Please note that "used" books without covers have, in most cases, been stolen. Neither the author nor the publisher has made any money on these books because they were supposed to be pulped for lack of sales.

Please do not purchase books without covers.